Shoreline of Infinity

Issue 17 Winter/Spring 2020

Award-winning science fiction magazine

published in Scotland for the Universe.

ISSN 2059-2590

ISBN 978-1-9993331-7-1

© 2020 Shoreline of Infinity.

Contributors retain copyright of own work.

Shoreline of Infinity is available in digital and print editions.

Submissions of fiction, art, reviews, poetry, non-fiction are welcomed: visit the website to find out how to submit.

www.shorelineofinfinity.com

Publisher

Shoreline of Infinity Publications / The New Curiosity Shop

Edinburgh

Scotland

170120

Contents

Cover: Siobhan McDonald

Shoreline of Infinity
Science Fiction Magazine
Editorial Team
Co-founder, Editor-in-Chief & Editor:
Noel Chidwick

Co-founder, Art Director:
Mark Toner

Deputy Editor & Poetry Editor:
Russell Jones

Reviews Editor:
Samantha Dolan

Non-fiction Editor:
Pippa Goldschmidt

Copy editors:
Andrew J Wilson, Iain Maloney,
Russell Jones, Pippa Goldschmidt

Manifold thanks to: Richard Ridgwell

First Contact
www.shorelineofinfinity.com

contact@shorelineofinfinity.com

Twitter: @shoreinf

and on Facebook

Pull up a Log

Congratulations to Ruth EJ Booth, who won the prize for best non-fiction at the 2019 British Fantasy Society's awards for her Noise and Sparks column. She continues to deserve the prefix 'award-winning', and you can pick up on her thoughts on page 103 with *The Elephant in the Ceremony Room*.

Congratulations also go to Simon Fung, who won the 2019 Flash Fiction prize with his story, *Those who live by the shawarma*: I shall never look at a kebab in the same way again. Congratulations too to our runners-up, Emma Levin and Anna Ziegelgoh. This year the judges were students of English Literature at Edinburgh University, who were as sharp as tacks at their task.

Sadly we have to report on the death last year of Martyn Turner. Martyn was one of Shoreline of Infinity's greatest fans. He was a subscriber from issue 1 and became a patreon as he felt it was important to support ventures like ours which provides opprtunities for new science fiction talents. Martyn was a regular at Event Horizon, always cheerful and a pleasure to talk to. The world needs more Martyns, not fewer.

We dedicate this issue of Shoreline of Infinity to the memory of Martyn Turner.

This issue has our usual mix of writers from all over the world, from Scotland, England, United States and Iran. But we begin with a story from a Shoreline regular, Netherlands writer Bo Balder. The title of her story, *The Elephant Keeper*, picks up from where we started with award-winning Ruth EJ Booth's piece.

—*Noel Chidwick, Editor-in-Chief*
January 2020

The Elephant Keeper

Bo Balder

London should have been a marvel. Steam cars barrelled through town and exogaian ships travelled to the Moon, Venus and Mars. But I was going under fast, living on streets full of soldiers returning from the Boer wars, without money, a place to stay or a job.

My elephant Mitzi had died, and the circus had no reason to keep me on without her. I'm no stranger to hard work, but I hadn't been able to find any kind of congenial employment. They'd laughed me away at the Zoo for being female and a gypsy. I was for the workhouse or the back streets if I didn't find a job soon.

The advertisement simply stated they needed *an experienced zookeeper, lrg. anim. pref'd, 25 pounds a year*. When I rang the bell at the Hampstead mansion, my feet sore from trudging the six miles from south London, I was shaking with hunger.

I followed a footman through the mansion's gardens to the Menagerie. We passed a sluggish lion, mangy monkeys and bleached-looking flamingos. The footman brought me to an unkempt, surly old gaffer. "This is James, his lordship's Zookeeper. He will decide on the hiring."

James seemed exactly like our old lion tamer Antoine, a mean, sloppy drunk. I'd never blamed Simba for taking Antoine's head off. James scratched his oily hair and shifted his tobacco quid around in his mouth. "Right, then. This way." He led me past more cages, all of them rank with droppings and old straw. Lazy sod.

The zebra, the baboons and the tapir rooted listlessly. You've got to give animals something to do. Circus animals work for a living, not just performing, they all have jobs in hauling and lifting and they get rewarded for them.

We stopped before an outsize cage with thicker-than-normal bars. It smelled odd. I couldn't put a name or face to these strange tangs of bitter and sweet and sour, and I've seen a lot of exotic animals pass through the circus. A heap of something indefinable lay among the rotting straw covering the plank floor. Shadows seemed to hover over it, making it hard to focus on its shape.

James spat out brown phlegm. "That's it. Bugger's dying. Ugly as hell, doesn't do much. But the guvnor likes it, coz it's exogaian. From the Moon or summat." He looked at me sideways from his bloodshot eyes.

"From the Moon?"

"That Frenchman, Jools Vern, brought 'em back with his ether ship."

I'd heard about that. Our clowns had performed a skit about Jules Verne and his exogaian wife.

"Vern sold the critters to his lordship before he disappeared under the sea. But it's not been worth the money. Just lies there moping," James said.

In my experience, a moping animal usually has good reason to do so. I just needed to find out what. "Does it eat grass and such, or does it eat meat?"

He looked at me as if I were barmy. "It's a critter, like a pig. I feeds it slops, like all proper critters." He turned and made to stomp off.

"Am I hired, then, Mr. James?"

He shrugged. "See anyone else wants to do it?" He disappeared among the cages.

I stood undecided for moment. But then again, I was destitute and alone, and at least he offered me a roof over my head and regular meals.

If I could keep whatever was in that cage *alive*.

I hoiked up my new uniform. The creature's presence made me feel peculiar. I kept wiping my hands on my pinny, but they were still sticky.

James had kept me busy all morning sweeping straw in the other cages, but now I could start getting to know my main charge. If I closed my eyes, the smells were just like the circus.

I sat down on the empty slops bucket. "I want to help you. Get to know you. I worked in a circus before. I love elephants, and Mitzi the most. But she died. Maybe from grief, because her child was sold off and the other one died. Who knows with elephants? But I had to leave the circus after because I had no act anymore."

I paused. I was sure the creature was listening, and I needed a less harrowing topic. If not for its sake, then for mine. It appeared a bit more present and aware than before, but it still made me feel odd. One moment it seemed to fill the whole cage, the next it seemed about my own size. The sense of itching dread came and went.

"I do miss the circus, though. Mitzi and Simba – he's the bad-tempered lion – and Hora and Joey, the baby elephants. And Prancer and Dancer and Joy and Jumper, the horses. And director Sferracavallo was always kind to me. He took me in, named me after his mother, even though I'm a gypsy. Amelia Sferracavallo, that's me. Treated me like a daughter. But then he turned me off with nothing when Mitzi died." I swallowed. Why couldn't I keep it bloody cheerful?

When it didn't react, I laid out some oats, clover and hay. A thick grey trunk wiggled out snaky fast and flicked over to the first heap of fodder. Its speed surprised me, but I collected myself and moved closer to have a better look. It held still, quivering. I felt a wave of fear crash through my body, touching first my stomach, then the skin of my face, leaving my forehead tight and dripping with sweat.

I wanted to be patient with it but couldn't. It seemed likely to die at any moment, which would cost me my job and any chance I had of ever returning to the circus.

I breathed out to calm myself, and hopefully the animal as well.

"Let me see you," I crooned. "I won't harm you. Come to me."

I took another step forward.

A great bulk reared up. Its shape was formless; huge, undulating masses of pockmarked grey hide, dry and brittle in most places, oozing and moist from straight slashes all over it. If it simply dropped down on me it would crush me to a pulp. It had no eyes or mouth, no legs or flippers, nothing, not even a trunk like before. For moments we hung in the balance; it poised to squelch me, I poised to run. Scents and feelings crashed through me like surf, swelling and retreating.

Swallowing, thinking of the distrustful lion in the circus, I put my hands down on the mottled gray hide. It felt cool, brittle, writhing where I'd expected hot and rough. A wave of feeling rose up in me. I'd been abandoned in this heavy place, I burned as if in a fire, under light that was too bright and sounds that were too harsh. Each breath crawled in thick and hot and disgusting.

I almost stepped back, fighting a rising nausea, but I knew I had to stand firm. "I'm sorry you feel that way. This must be a strange world to you. I'll do what I can to help you."

The air was so taut it almost twanged. I pictured sheets hung over the cage, hosing it down with water to cool it. The idea of water made it cringe away under my palm.

"No water, then. I'll see about some shade for you. Now be a good boy and sniff this food. You might even like some of it."

The tension snapped like a rotten hair band.

The creature fell away from my hand and shrank down, crumpling in on itself. My fear evaporated. The snout or fingertip or whatever it was nosed delicately from leaf to leaf. It retreated after the last herb. I sensed exhaustion and disappointment. I waited for a long time, but it sent me no more feelings.

The next day, when I was just done sweeping, I heard voices approaching from the house. I took my broom to the already swept floor. Masters like to see their servants work.

But when I looked up again, casual-like, the small troupe approaching through the Menagerie was a far grander sort of people than a mere head Zookeeper. The Marquess was an elderly gentleman in morning suit, clean shaven with caterpillar eyebrows, accompanied by lesser gents and a very tall floating lady. Floating?

When they ambled closer – the ladies with scented handkerchiefs before their noses, the gents with flasks of liquor in their hands – I made a deep curtsey.

The floating lady kept drawing my eye. She wasn't actually floating; she was being wheeled around on a dolly like a stack of luggage. She was strapped on tightly, right over her mutton-sleeved dress of purple bombazine and striped underskirt. Did the Marquess fear her running off, or flying away? She didn't seem to have wings.

A black veil obscured her face, but her complexion shone through floridly. Even discounting the luggage cart, she was enormously tall, topping His Lordship by a head.

"You may close your mouth now, Zookeeper," the Marquess said. "How fares the critter?"

I curtseyed again. "Better, my lord. I'm feeding it up, as you see."

His eyes roamed around the neatly swept cage and back to me. "It had better shape up. Hasn't done a bally thing but slouch and pong since I bought the three of them."

Three? Had the creature's mate or children died, perhaps?

"Get it to show us some tricks or it's off to the knackers'. Carry on."

He could sack me with a snap of his fingers. A mere nod, even. I had to produce results and quickly.

"As you see, Lady Ptarthis," one of the less important men in the entourage started, "the vermiform's innate adaptability to Terrestrial gravitation is inferior to yours, as I've set out in *Eindeutige Beschreibung der Würmer von Mons Olympus*. It is your splendid will and courage that set an example to us all."

"You are too kind, Doctor Ssschmidt," a deep resounding voice spoke from behind the veil. Lady Ptarthis sounded more like a booming underwater creature than an ordinary woman. And hadn't the doctor just implied she was also an exogaian? I couldn't be sure because of those strange words he used. Her face was very red, indeed. I checked for a strip of skin between her gloves or at her neck, but she was completely covered up.

As if she had felt my gaze, she flicked up her veil and gave me a look. My skin goosebumped from my neck down to my calves, and my hands turned cold. It last only a second, then she was covered again. I couldn't recall seeing her face at all.

At the servants' dinner in the kitchen that night, I asked about getting herbs from the kitchen garden. "For the creature. It's my job to feed it and it won't eat."

Cook ladled the plate next to me extra high. I sat between the footman who'd wheeled the exogaian lady and my boss, which meant more scrutiny.

"Those herbs are for people, not animals," she said and gave me a serving of fragrant stew. She knew how to put a sprig of rosemary to good use, she did. "Forward girl."

I put my head down and ate, hoping they'd forget about me.

The footman pinched my elbow. I jabbed him in the ribs. His hand crept to my thigh, but I didn't want to attract more attention by slapping him.

"Ask Lady Ptarthis," he breathed into my ear, tickling mightily. "She's very interested in the creature. Visits it every night."

She sounded like a very odd lady, even for someone who came from the Moon. Getting carted around like a traveller's trunk, sneaking around at night to visit the creature. I wondered what she was up to. Nothing good, I bet.

Maybe Lady P. knew what the creature needed to eat, her being from the same place. And if she visited it every night, well, that smoothed the way for a chat. I wasn't sure if she was fiancée or mistress or something different altogether, but in neither case could I ask for an audience with her, could I? But at night, I could sneak out and wait for her in the cage.

After dinner we servants trooped up to our rooms in the attic. The little maids were asleep as soon as they hit their beds, so I stuffed my old clothes in the bed, nicked their candle ends and snuck downstairs. Cook sat nodding in front of the fire and never roused as I tiptoed past her.

The Menagerie was quiet, its hunched structures black against the colorless night sky. No light burned in Mr. James' cottage. The animals snuffled and sighed.

"It's all right, Mr. Zebra, only me. Go back to sleep." Maybe I should steal the zebra instead of the creature. Probably easier. But also less extraordinary.

I opened the door to the creature's cage. Something twitched in the straw. It hadn't done that any of the earlier times I'd entered. Was it because of the night? I should have brought a lamp; the stubs of candle wouldn't cast light past my own feet.

I stepped closer. "It's me, Amelia."

It stirred. I sank down on my haunches. My fingertips felt rough hot hide, but it flinched away from me immediately. I contained my sigh and let out a long slow breath. Animals notice impatience.

I sat down. I could stay awake a whole night. There had been plenty of opportunity for me to take breaks, as Mr. James wasn't a very vigilant overseer.

I left my hand where it was. I pretended I was sitting on the perch of my old wagon, with a bottle of wine and a cigar, looking up at the stars, with the smells of crushed herbs, the sound of crickets or someone playing the violin. Letting the horse walk at its own pace, enjoying just such a late spring night.

I felt the creature inching closer. After what seemed like a very long time, maybe as much as half an hour, its skin touched me. I felt the same roughness and lack of body warmth as before. I didn't speak, just sat there, letting it get the sense of me, waiting for the next move. I knew it would come, although maybe not tonight. I could simply start sleeping here, better than in the stuffy attic.

I almost did fall asleep, but then the creature jerked its appendage away from me. I sat up straight. A faint screeching and crunching sounded. Wheels over gravel. I withdrew quietly to the darkest corner of the cage, as far from the creature as I could get.

I waited and sure enough, the funny cart arrived, with Lady Ptarthis on it like an upright portmanteau. Pushed by the same footman who'd alerted me to her night-time outings. An oil lamp hanging from the top of the cart threw dancing shadows over the gravel and the sleeping lion.

The footman wheeled her to the cage entrance and assisted her off the cart. She leaned heavily on him, as if she were infirm or old. The atmosphere in the cage changed, becoming charged with fear and something else, something bright and eager. I thought the fear was the creature's, and the eagerness originated with Lady Ptarthis.

The footman took a chair from the back of the cart and set it up near the creature, at what I thought of as its hindquarters. I wanted to get further back into the darkest part of the cage, but the back wall stopped me. I tried to breathe without sound.

Ptarthis clambered into the cage, as slow and careful as if she was eighty. The footman held her up while she clung to the door jambs, and then one shaky half-crouching step took her to the chair. She collapsed on it as if her weight was too much for her to carry. She was tall and slender, looking as if she had no strength in her back at all. Maybe she was sick.

The footman pushed the chair with Ptarthis in it closer to the creature. I heard a snick and something shiny caught the light of the oil lantern. A knife? Whatever for?

The footman brushed the straw from the exogaian creature. Its dark bulk seemed dull under the yellowy lantern, inert, no limbs or trunks visible. I wondered why it was so afraid. Ptarthis lifted the knife with another flicker of light on metal and wielded it horizontally. It sounded like a fish being filleted. My skin cringed away from the burning pain as the knife cut through the hide. It was strange, half-seeing it happen in the wavering light of the oil lamp, having to guess at it, and at the same time feeling someone cutting into me - into it. It was all I could do not to cry out and wrench myself away from the knife.

Ptarthis brought a glistening piece of stuff to her mouth. I noticed only now that she wasn't veiled. There wasn't enough light to have a good look at her features. The wash of the oil lamp on a gleaming cheekbone and pointy teeth didn't reassure me. The sharp teeth tore at the wet dark thing she held up.

Ptarthis devoured about half the fillet in big tearing bites. The creature's flesh must be quite tender, or perhaps she didn't chew, just swallow, like many big predators. Then she handed the remainder to the footman, who held it two feet away from his body.

I must have made some kind of sound after all, maybe a little gasp.

"Ssooo," she said. "Who'ss there?"

I said nothing. It might be to both our advantages to pretend neither of us had ever been here. She jerked the lantern from the footman's hand and swung it round to the back of the cage. "Reveal yourself!"

I pushed myself upright and took a small step forward. "It's the Zookeeper, Milady."

Large gold eyes blinked at me. I read no comprehension in them.

"I take care of the creature, Milady."

"That's right," the footman said.

Ptarthis thrust the lantern back at him without taking her eyes off me. He stumbled backwards.

I felt like a rabbit caught in a snake's gaze - and no sooner had I thought it, then I remembered the width of her jaw and her hissing speech. Perhaps Lady Ptarthis had some sinuous forebears, as we were supposed to have monkeys swinging from branch to branch.

She beckoned me to her. I obeyed, not sure if it was against my will. As I inched closer, I smelled an odd, vaguely disturbing scent. It reminded me a bit of the creature, but it was sharper, more savage. Dry, dusty, maybe a hint of sulphur.

When I thought myself still safely out of reach, she stretched out an immensely long, thin arm and yanked me closer by my apron. Her hand twisted and clamped my breast. I gasped in surprise, not least at the answering warmth in my belly. The footman made a strangled noise. The light from the oil lamp diminished. He must have turned away from us. No help there.

We froze, Ptarthis and I, she with my breast in her hand. It was a large hand, and my bosom not quite a handful. I didn't know what to do. Perhaps this was normal behavior among her class. What did I know? In the circus we had men who were known to visit each other's wagons. I had heard rumors about women who did the same.

So I stood fast and returned the intense look from her round yellow eyes, although I couldn't begin to guess what her half-seen facial expressions meant. She pulled me closer, and I yielded to minimize the pain.

She rent my pinafore with one sharp-tipped finger. I gulped.

"I could just take my dress off, Milady," I said. "I'd rather not be punished for ruining a perfectly good garment."

Lady Ptarthis didn't speak, but removed her claw from the neck of my borrowed dress. I loosened it as quickly as I could, determined to keep my eyes on her and not think about the footman. The situation was dangerous and embarrassing enough without taking him into account. I unbuttoned my blouse and bodice, leaving my back covered in hopes of getting some clothes back on as quickly as possible. I unhooked my skirts and then stood there in my bloomers and naked chest, shivering, though the night was warm.

I think Ptarthis retracted the clawed nails, because I felt only soft fingertips as she prodded and poked me all over. She seemed especially fascinated by any fat-covered, more cushiony bits, of which I had but a few modest ones, having only recently started to eat proper meals again. I tried to keep my teeth from chattering.

She lifted her hand to my breast, supporting herself on the back of the chair, and tweaked my nipple. It hurt, and to my surprise, she stopped.

With a wave of her free hand, she invited me to lie down. I was too afraid not to comply. In spite of my decision not to, I couldn't help a quick glance towards the footman's back. It was rigid, and he stared off into the distance, though his breath might have been a trifle heavy.

I supported the Lady Ptarthis in her tortuous attempts lie down next to me. She hissed in pain as her knees hit the floor of the cage.

She put a hot dry hand on my thigh and proceeded upwards. I lay stiff and uncomfortable at first, wondering why she was doing this. I'd expected to be asked to perform a duty such as she was performing on me – why was it the other way around? As long as I could think clearly, before new and not unpleasant sensations swept me, I thought hard.

She needed the creature. I needed the creature.

Her cooperation might provide me with a chance to bring a crowd-pleasing animal to the circus. I might go home again. As for Ptarthis, she could be gotten rid of somehow.

The creature lay sluggish all day. An air of satisfaction emanated from it, which I contemplated incessantly. Had Ptarthis not maimed the creature? But instead it seemed better rather than worse.

The next few weeks slithered by in a daze of waiting for the pinch of my elbow at the dinner table. That was how the footman signaled I was to be present in the cage at night.

I don't know why I went each time, but I did. And as soon as Ptarthis was wheeled up, crunching over the nighttime gravel, I'd quiver like a bowstring, because soon after the filleting knife she'd come to me and touch me. I wished to be with her every night, but truth was I needed my sleep. I became as sluggish as the creature by day. It snoozed safely under its straw, I leaned on my broom and catnapped.

I worked hard but didn't seem to be able to gain weight. Even Cook, not a softhearted woman by the most giving of definitions, piled my plate higher and slipped me buttered bread between meals.

One of the upper maids said Ptarthis wasn't his lordship's plaything, he was hers. That she'd bailed him out of a boatload of debts and consequently he did her bidding in everything. She must have come down on the exogaian ship with more than her weight in jewelry or gold, the servants speculated. But Cook said it wasn't true. The Marquess had bought the creature, Ptarthis and another as a lot, all three together. Scandalized the whole household, it did.

"Just a kept woman," Cook said and sniffed definitively.

"You coming down with something?" Mr. James asked. "The help these days, ruddy weaklings."

I stood with bowed head, but at this question I straightened up and tried to look perky. "Healthy as a horse, guv," I said. "Never get sick."

Something was sapping my strength. If I didn't want to keel over or get the sack, I couldn't wait any longer to make my move. Next dinner, I breathed my request into the footman's ear.

The next day, after having gulped down a second helping of blancmange, and feeling overfull because of it, I was summoned to the drawing room. Lady Ptarthis wished to speak to me. A spike of guilt mixed with hope stabbed me in the stomach and my cheeks grew hot. This could go so many ways.

I stood up and smoothed my poorly repaired pinafore. I didn't sense much sympathy from the other servants as I made to leave the kitchen. I was too new, I supposed, with a job that was too different.

The between maid showed me into the small drawing room off the great hall. Lady Ptarthis reclined on a chaise-longue, another 'tweenie' fanning her face. She dismissed them both and beckoned me closer. She was dressed in a loose silk gown and bed jacket dripping with lace and beads. In spite of this informal attire, she also wore a tiara, several rows of necklaces, twenty or so bracelets, a pair of long earrings and something shiny around her waist.

I'd heard from the other servants she never touched her food, never ate anything at all. They wondered.

I thought I knew.

As I navigated between aspidistras and side tables laden with porcelain figurines, sweat broke out all over my face, my scalp prickled, I was close to vomiting. Only by exercising the strongest willpower could I make myself walk up to Ptarthis, but I couldn't close the last two yards. I hadn't felt like that in the cage last night.

Ptarthis's alien face remained impassive, or at least I detected no sign of emotion in her fierce, snake-like eyes.

"Come to me."

"Yes, Milady," I mumbled, swaying, black spots before my eyes. I clenched my muscles harder. It must be Ptarthis who was causing this dread. But I was no rabbit, and I didn't plan to be eaten.

"Closer," she rasped.

I stepped closer, swaying dizzily. Her widespread fingers hovered over my belly, almost but not quite touching. I felt no sicker, but no better either.

"I have a proposal for you," I croaked out. "The creature is dying here. I can take it somewhere it can be looked after and get healthy again."

"Ah," she said.

I waited. She didn't blink or move.

"I thought…I thought you cared for it. I thought you might pay for the journey to the circus. To France."

"Sir-kus?"

"Bright place, many lights?"

"House."

"I suppose so, Milady."

I waited, the fear that I might throw up growing stronger, steadied by the fear of touching her if I fell.

"Where is France?"

"On the continent, Milady. Across the sea."

Her lip curled. "Water? Can we fly?"

I stared. "I don't have wings, Milady. Do you?"

Her mouth opened wide, soundlessly. Was she laughing? "I approve plan. I will accompany. We leave here. Go far away from Marquess. With you. You please me."

I shuddered, whether from fear or delight I couldn't say. I'd been preparing for such a request, of course, since I'd calculated she couldn't survive without the creature, but it still seemed a lot to pay. But my return to the circus was worth a few unnatural acts.

"It will cost money, Milady," I said. "Do you have any?"

She fished a stack of bills and a pouch full of guineas out of her purse and showed them to me. "That is money, yes? Enough?"

I swallowed and said it was.

"He footman will arrange travel to boat. You arrange travel to bright place."

She pushed me away and stretched out her long, sinuous body in the slanting rays of the evening sun.

I popped out of the door like a Jack-in-the-box, light-headed with relief. I leaned against the wall. I ought to have removed myself from the hall immediately, so none of the family would have to encounter me, but I needed a moment.

"She takes you like that, doesn't she? And the men don't notice a thing," the little between maid said, stepping out of the covered door that led to the servants' passages. "Come in, quickly. I hear people coming up the stairs."

Ptarthis hadn't sickened me like that in the cage. And how did the Marquess stand her presence if this was her usual effect on people?

I followed the maid to the attic, lay down on the bed in my shift and thought. The footman was going to arrange travel to Dover and across the channel. Then I'd have to find the circus. In spring they traveled the coasts of Belgium and France to serve the rich clientele that took the sea air in Knokke and Deauville.

I asked the butler for a sheet of paper and a stamp to write to the ringmaster, my adopted father Giuseppe Sferracavallo. He'd have to take me back if I brought the creature. I only had to find a way to manage all this in secrecy and without letting Ptarthis know she'd never reach France. She was wealthy and well-respected. I needed the creature more than she did.

Once we arrived in Dover, I left the sleeping Lady Ptarthis in her cabin on the *Dover Dilly* and snuck on board the *Master of Calais*. I'd arranged passage on it for the creature, also via the footman. Easy to guess for what payment.

I walked the creature to the loading dock. I clamped my hands around the bars of the cage. "How are you doing?" I asked.

It returned a wordless calm.

I whispered my goodbyes and stumbled to my cabin, feeling worse with every pitching set of stairs I had to climb. My shabby day clothes got me a few looks, especially when I went into Second Class.

I opened the cabin door and looked straight into Ptarthis's giant yellow orbs. She sat on the tiny chair wedged in between the bunks and the washstand.

I gasped. Or perhaps even screamed, for it seemed I heard an echo of a heartrending screech in the air.

She bared her double rows of pointy teeth. "Did we not agree travel to continent together, Amelia?"

I grasped at the straws of my dignity. "Of course we did. I did not expect you in a Second Class cabin, is all."

She raised her brow in a perfect imitation of a highborn lady's disapproval. "No lie. I know."

My cheeks burned when I realized she'd probably got her information from the footman in return for the same services she granted me. Ptarthis waited, patiently, inhumanly still, not even blinking those enormous eyes, until I had collected my wits.

"Right. Will you let me get my things?" I said. I felt numb, resigned to whatever might happen. She'd cast me off without a penny, or worse, give me over to the Gendarmes. Gone were my chances of a new life within the circus. I'd never find a better substitute for my dear Mitzi than the creature.

"Come," she said.

She preceded me out of the door, stooping through the low doorway. A steward stood waiting with a push-chair. He walked her through the still heaving corridors with me following for lack of alternatives. The ship was on the open sea, there was nowhere to go. On dry land I could have run for it, although being a fugitive is not enjoyable. One is cold, hungry and thirsty, and continually afraid. I didn't look forward to trying it again. My weeks at the Marquess' had made me realize how wonderful it was to have a safe place to sleep and a full belly.

Instead of rising up to the First Class Deck and the captain, or any kind of officer, we descended. I followed mutely, too stunned to even wonder where we were going.

I realized I'd descended these stairs before, when I'd been looking for the creature. It was easier by day, although one could now see the shabbiness and disrepair of the ship. We were going to the cargo hold.

As we approached the crate, my physical discomfort lessened. My head cleared, I was no longer nauseous, and my legs felt steadier. Now I knew I was afraid, not sick. Very afraid. I just didn't know of what. Ptarthis wouldn't hurt me, right? And I didn't think the creature could.

The steward put a brake on the push chair, received something out of Ptarthis' purse for his trouble and left with a bow.

When I put my hand on the crate, an odd feeling assailed me. At first an enormous relief when the nausea of Ptarthis' presence was lifted completely. Then there was giddiness, like the first drink, or the anticipation of great pleasure. The fear was gone, although my stomach still felt peculiar.

I leant my forehead against the plank until I'd steadied. I cast my eyes up to Ptarthis.

A stray beam of sunlight caught her copper skin and lent it radiance. Her golden eyes smiled down at me and I shivered at the memory of pleasure by her talons and tongue. She was gorgeous. I wanted to lean into her breast to inhale her fragrance, to bask in her presence.

I remembered my lack of repulsion for her, that first night with the creature, and now, and the discomfort with Ptarthis when it hadn't been present. Why was that?

"I feed it," Ptarthis said.

The creature sent me approval and pleasure. And at last I understood. The Marquess had said there had been three of them originally, and I hadn't understood that he'd meant not three creatures, but Ptarthis, the creature and a third person or being.

It had never wanted to be alone with me; in fact, it couldn't. It needed someone to sustain it, as Ptarthis needed it to eat. I was to be the necessary third party in the triad, to replace the one that had died. I was the only one who could eat and drink on this world. In return, they would make me happy. Ptarthis would give me physical joy, the creature mental pleasure. It would make me able to bear Ptarthis' proximity.

I was trapped. I couldn't move for the delicious languor they imposed upon me, but my mind was running around like a mouse on a wheel. I recalled my fear of a minute ago, but it wasn't as real as the joyous expectation of Ptarthis' embrace.

"We should still join the circus," I said, albeit with a moan. "There is no better place for you to remain undetected, if that is what you wish. Although I cannot see why you left the Marquess."

Ptarthis moved her brows. In the light of the sunbeam I could see they were painted on. Did she have any body hair at all? The speculation caused a shudder down my spine and I had to close my eyes.

"He man," Ptarthis hissed. "Wanted me to bow him. I bow no man."

Ha. She could talk. She hadn't had to bow to bloody Mr. James and every other man I'd ever met.

"So are we agreed? We find my circus, and we can live a good life."

I didn't mind being the mistress of an alien creature that much. If I could have my place in the circus, with a grand animal to draw punters, I'd be happy. Ptarthis could do worse than sit in a booth and be the snake woman. There could be nothing wrong with this prospect whatsoever.

"This is agreed," Ptarthis said. "We will be free and enjoy each other."

The creature added a shot of bliss to my already whitening thoughts.

Bo lives and works close to Amsterdam. Bo is the first Dutch author to have been published in F&SF. Clarkesworld, Analog and other places. Her SF novel *The Wan* was published by Pink Narcissus Press. When not writing, she knits, reads and gardens, preferably all three at the same time.
For more about her work, you can visit her website or find Bo on Facebook.

The Weavers

S.A.M. Rundell

The heat's made people fucking fruity. It's not supposed to be this hot. Not this late at night. Not in Paisley.

Fucking global warming shite.

It's late now and the heat's worn off a bit, but not its effects on the Fruit & Nut bars of Causeyside Street. Me and Wully slow up a bit as we come down the hill by the Town Hall. This is partly because Wully's getting on and hills are a bastard for him, and partly because the polis are up ahead corralling a group of youths

Art: Jackie Duckworth

in shorts, distinct now in two opposing groups, drunk on sun and White Lightning. Montagues and Capulets they are not.

An older man ahead of us, bearded and sunburnt, shakes his head as he crosses the road.

"Paisley!" he shouts, raising his arms to the straight-backed officers, the gesticulating youths and curious onlookers, "City of fucking culture!"

I look at Wully and he hitches up his eyebrows, gestures with his stick.

We take up the Threads, drawing in the yellow light, and the heat, the clack of tottering high-heels and the brash confidence of a skinny youth with his top off. I pull on a Thread gently. It buzzes electric as I twine it with the bits of pride at our bid for City of Culture; bits of hope disguised as sullen, eye-rolling apathy, and some fine delicate strands of quiet ambition. It makes for a nice wee Weave, that. Sort of sweet and sour.

Wully nods again and we move on.

We stop at the traffic lights. Karaoke music's coming from the pub ahead. Wully leans against the railings for a moment and we wait for the green man, even though there's no cars coming. His breathing is heavy and part of me wants to Weave this Thread. This moment, here: a dying man on a balmy Paisley night, shaking his head at the off-key caterwauling coming from the pub. I have a keen sense for these things; we all do. I know the moments that need to be part of the Tapestry. But this moment is not mine to Weave.

The green man blinks on and we cross the road.

The 'City of Culture' banners don't make it this far up Neilston Road. No #wTeamPaisley up this neck of the woods. This is Rab's patch. He Weaves here between his trips to the multiple chemists and drug dealers on the street. Dave takes over up by Glenburn and Craw Road, posh nob that he is. Wully's battle ground was the town centre, keeping the mills and the cobbles, the Abbey, the Coats, the statues in check. It would be my patch soon.

"Wully, I can call us a taxi, you know," I say, as he slows again.

"I know, son. But I want a pint." I hesitate and he reads my silence and chuckles wheezily. "I'm no gonnie fall down deid, lad. Come on, buy me a pint with that fancy non-contact thingamy."

"Contactless?"

He grumbles and steers the way into the bar that is crowded and noisy and smells of sweat. I order our drinks while Wully finds us a seat, or rather while Wully hangs around looking lost until someone takes pity on him and offers him their table.

I Weave a little while I wait at the bar. There's laughter and excitement; the heady enjoyment of a Saturday night in the warm. "Aye, hotter than Spain. Look!" says one red-faced man, brandishing a cracked iPhone at his pal. "Hotter that Spain!"

I take bits and pieces and twine them with some old memories of a fug of cigarette smoke, rainy days of sleet and smur.

"Bit on the nose," comments Wully after I join him again.

"I was just doodling," I say. "Besides, I let the Weave go. This is Rab's patch."

"Doesn't mean you cannie work here, lad."

"Aye, but it's manners, in't it."

He smirks and takes a sip of his drink. He takes off his thick glasses and polishes them on the edge of his t-shirt.

'If you think something's worth recording, there's no harm in it. Anyhow, do you really think Rab would mind?"

It's true. Rab may have been an addict but he's also the kindest man I know. Yas on the other hand...she would mind. Fucking princess.

"You're responsible for them now, Malcolm," says Wully, watching me closely. "And they'll respect you, son. You've got... what's the word...gravitas."

I laugh loudly. "You're a funny bastard, Wully. But nah," I take a swig of beer. "They'll no respect me the same as they do you."

"That's cus I'm an old fucker," says Wully. "Age does that tae ye; just you wait."

I laugh again and sigh deeply.

"Now, there's something you might want tae look at," he says nodding surreptitiously.

There's a middle-aged couple sitting in a corner. They're both drunk but they can't take their eyes off each other. They're holding hands under the table and giggling like teenagers. I smile a little and roll my eyes at Wully. "Dirty bastard," I say, but pull a Thread all the same, wrapping their giddy romance with the heat of summer; childhoods spent up the Braes or fishing in the Cart.

"Nicely done."

"Aye, I'm no fucking amateur," I say smiling, "Got to fill your old-man shoes, don't I?"

We finish our drinks and move on. The sky is inky and the air is close. There's excitement here, like an orchestra tuning up or the title cards of a classic film. We walk slowly behind two men staggering bravely across the road. Some kids run around a corner, up past their bedtime, heading for Brodie Park to smoke, drink, giggle till their sides hurt and drag long and hard on the indestructible fag-end of youth. I consider pulling the Threads they leave behind but I realise I couldn't do them justice. I don't feel indestructible. The night, pregnant with possibilities, to me just seems like the end of something.

I glance over at Wully who deftly pulls up the Threads and knits them together, simple and tight. There's no sadness...Jesus fuck, there's not even old age. It's impossible to Weave objectively, but the old bastard's captured it with the pure memory of youth. I feel old and inadequate.

"Show-off," I mutter.

I can smell barbecue smoke coming from somewhere. It's incongruous and somehow necessary.

"So, if I take over the Town Centre," I say, "and train up Wee Katie... where do you want her to work when she's ready?"

"That'll be up to you, son," says Wully, "and up to her."

"Aye, I thought you'd say that," I say with a sigh. "I suppose we'll know when we know, eh?"

"Aye."

I glance up and notice the windows thrown wide open; I can see a silhouette at one of them, cigarette smoke drifting out against the darkening sky.

We meet in Eileen's house. Her kids are at their dad's tonight and she's tidied up special. The others are already here.

"Kettle's on, boys," Eileen says as Wully and I sit in the drooping but clean sofa. "Malcolm, gonnie give out they coasters," she says to me.

"Coasters? Very posh, Eileen," says Dave.

"Bit rich coming from you," I say, "you big PACE wanker."

Dave smacks my head with a coaster but Yasmin gets in the way before I can retaliate, taking Dave's vacated seat. "Is this gonnie take long? I'm opening the shop tomorrow."

"Come on, Yas. You could do that in your sleep," says Dave, frisbeeing a coaster at Wee Katie who tries to catch it, misses, blushes a pure beamer and goes to help Eileen in the kitchen.

"Take that as a compliment, hen," says Wully, shifting to get comfy on the sofa. "You work hard in that shop, a seen ye at it."

"Thanks Wully," she sways with a pointed glare at Dave.

"So here, how's Wee Katie?" I mutter to Wully. "She ready?"

"She's nervous, aye. But she'll do fine,"

"She's a nice wee lassie," says Yasmin, flicking her hair over a shoulder. "Dead polite."

" 'Course she is, she's ma granddaughter," says Wully, smiling only a little sadly.

Eileen comes back in carrying a tray of mugs and a plate of caramel wafers. Wee Katie trailing in her wake perches on the arm of the sofa.

"No sign of Rab yet?" says Eileen, checking her watch.

"He'll be here," I say and just as I do there's a knock on the door and Eileen goes to open it, leaving only the faintest trace of the chippy where she works.

It's Rab, who shuffles in, his tracky evidently not bothering him in the heat of the night. He's carrying a blue carrier bag from which he produces some rich tea biscuits that he gives to Eileen. "Just a wee mindin'," he says. He fishes in the bag again and pulls out a battered paperback which he gives to Wee Katie, "Wully says you like reading so a brought you that. Huvnae read it mind, but ma next door neighbour says it's dead good."

"Thank you," says Wee Katie, taking the book. "You didnae huv to."

"Special day fur ye, hen," he says. I glance at Dave, who gives me a guilty shrug. None of us had brought a gift or a minding.

"Such a nice boy you are, Rab," says Eileen. "You have a wee seat and a cuppa."

Once the tea is finished and the plate is littered with scrunched-up foil wrappers we fall silent. No one has given any indication that we should; we've all decided that the moment has arrived. Wee Katie looks at the floor, twisting fingers in her lap.

Eileen pulls herself forward in her chair. "Right, no offence, yous lot, but a'v got work in the morning."

"Aye," agrees Dave, "If ... if that's ok with you, Wully."

Wully huffs and I nudge him gently in the ribs. "Aye, Davie boy," he says, "that's fine."

"Right then," says Eileen. I think she looks a bit weepy. "Wully. It's been an honour working with you," she says. She's about as used to making speeches as we are. Her knuckles tap gently on the arm of the chair. "You've taught all ae us here and...well, you'll be missed."

"Well that's bloody good to know," says Wully and we breathe out a laugh that is full of tension and sadness.

"Aye, well..." Eileen continues, "we're glad it's your wee Katie that's stepping up. You'll make a great addition to the team, hen," she says and Katie smiles.

"I hope so," she says, with a glance at her Grampa.

Wully gives her a pat on the arm and a wee grin. "You'll do fine, darlin'."

Silently, we share our Weaves: thousands of knitted Threads full of lives and voices; stone and rain; music and traffic. The layers run deep, thick with history: mills, and looms and floating fibres.

I breathe in, enjoying the feeling of everyone's Weaves out in the open. Wully's is fine and intricate, heavy with years of Paisley life. He pulls the Weave towards Wee Katie who's sitting cross-legged on the floor; she's concentrating, her face screwed up. I watch as she pulls a Thread. It's a nice thing, simple and innocent but full of expectation. It's got us all in it, this wee sitting room, the tea, the caramel wafers, Rab's paperback. It's got her Grampa and the lesson he's taught her and the lessons I'll be teaching her soon. Sweat beads on her brow now, as she takes the Thread and ties it to Wully's.

Wully smiles and casts off the last Thread, twining it with Katie's new one. It makes a lovely counterpoint for a second and then Wully's Weave becomes hers and she pulls it around her, wrapped momentarily in her future and her long distant past.

Sarah is a Paisley-based writer and lover of all things fantastical. She is proud of her hometown and everything it continues to do after some pretty tough times. When not writing, Sarah is a full time teacher of primary school children and is currently scrambling to finish her masters dissertation.

Community Service

Brian M. Milton

Graxnix staggered along the corridor muttering to themselves about missed opportunities as an alarm blared out of the speaker system. The insistent, repetitive note deet-deet-deeted into their brain, impelling them towards the control room. They slapped their second lefty on the hatchway as they entered.

"Do you need to make that horrible noise? I said I was on my way."

The alarm cut off and a bland computerised voice came from a grille set in the panel of blinking lights and screens at the front of the control room. "Experience over the one thousand, six hundred and ninety-seven community service missions I have operated has shown that offenders such as yourself are prone to laziness. I have ascertained that additional impetus early in the mission can help to get past this. Also it amuses me. Not something that often happens on these missions."

Graxnix slumped into a bucket chair, pulling all six of their limbs up and wrapping them around their body in a protective manner. "But I said I was coming and you can see I was."

Graxnix scowled at the grille and turned to look at the other chair in the control room where their fellow community service victim was slumped, idly flicking through images on a tablet. "I don't get you, Splagner, how can you take this? You look so relaxed."

Splagner waved their first righty dismissively in the air while their second righty held the tablet, their second lefty continued to flick through the images and their first lefty pulled a sweet-pop from their mouth to allow them to speak. "I've done this community service stuff enough times to know how it works, mate. The computer'll try to wind you up and the worst thing you can do is let it. The easiest way through this is to just do what it says, let it all wash over you and soon enough you'll be back in your favourite rock pool wrapping all six of your tentacles around whoever it is you like doing that with."

A brief burst of static came from the computer speaker which sounded to Graxnix almost like a sigh before the computer spoke again. "While I am glad you are intending to follow my orders, Splagner Gardont, I am disappointed in your cynicism and will be noting that in my report on you."

Splagner did not bother to pull the sweet-pop from their mouth this time and simply mumbled around it. "Whatever. Time served is all the court cares about."

The computer continued. "I have the first piece of detritus for you to pick up. My scanners have detected a manufactured metallic object that is travelling at a low velocity with no apparent propulsion. This makes it statistically likely to be a piece of flotsam and exactly the sort of thing that you should gather in. Make your way to the garbage collection bay and put on your pressure suits."

Graxnix slapped the side of the bucket chair. "Garbage collection? You mean you're actually going to make us pick it up? What do you need us for? Surely with all your AI programming and a simple tractor beam or remote tentacle you can bring it in yourself."

"I could, but that would not be you performing your community service. The courts have decreed that you will spend the next three months collecting detritus from the space lanes and you must serve that sentence. It is indubitably simpler to do this using my vast computing power and all that modern technology can supply but the point here is to punish you for your illegal drug misuse. Be assured that on the main routes, where a rogue asteroid or probe from a long-dead civilisation might actually endanger travellers, this operation is only carried out by competent artificial intelligences such as myself."

Splagner flowed out of the chair, pulling their body up on to its two lower tentacles, and looked over at Graxnix. "Don't sweat it, mate. It's so much easier than some of the community service programmes I've heard of. You don't want to be digging wells on a desert planet, now do you?"

Graxnix heaved themselves out of the bucket seat. They really wanted to tell the computer to stuff its community service, but Splagner was right. There were worse punishments than this and Graxnix did not want those. For one, their elder parent had threatened to pull Graxnix from university and sign them up for the Naval Cadets if they didn't come back with a good report and Graxnix had no doubt the old monster would do it. Graxnix had ridden their luck as far as they could with their parents and now had to get a good report from this community service to keep all three of the interfering busybodies happy.

Graxnix followed Splagner down the corridor. Watching the larger youth Graxnix couldn't help but admire them both for their relaxed attitude to the stupid jobs the computer wanted them to do and the way they flowed along. Splagner was permanently slumped, their torso so close to the floor that they used four limbs to propel them, none of them seeming to put much effort in. Their optical array was almost flat to its top and it all gave the impression of someone with almost no head. This reminded Graxnix of the lesser-evolved ancestor starfish that they'd seen in the zoo as a child. The ones with such a small brain it was buried in their bodies and not in a head standing proud. Of course, they were so far back down the evolutionary ladder that they still had digits all over their limbs that they used to move about and had not concentrated their sight cells in any useful manner at all. They also lay completely flat and used all six of their limbs to move – something Splagner looked constantly to be on the verge of copying.

The Garbage Collection Bay was an open hangar easily big enough to take a couple of ground cars with room to work on them. Beside the entrance were racks with spacesuits, which Graxnix and Splagner pulled on. On the far side was the hangar door, a whole wall that could open outwards by hydraulic piston. Just in front was a small console beside a large robotic tentacle that was connected to the wall. To the back of the bay were fold-out shelves and boxes to store the rubbish that they, as community service workers, were expected to collect. Rocks of various sizes and the odd piece of battered machinery, such as a torn solar panel or piece of heat shielding, occupied a few of the shelves and there was a large pile of rocks and rubbish too large for the shelves piled against the rear wall. "Initially you are advised to clip your safety line to the wall and then you will be evacuating the atmosphere before opening the bay door," said the computer.

Graxnix hurried over to the wall beside Splagner and the small console and found the safety line in a pouch at the suit's rear. They hooked it onto the wall with a satisfying thunk. As they did they heard Splagner's voice over the suit speaker, as quiet and relaxed as ever.

"Safety checks, please."

The computer replied in a lower volume than it had used to speak to Graxnix. "Suits sealed and operating correctly, Splagner Gardont. Proceed with opening the bay, and do ensure Graxnix Pindom is aware of the process."

"Sure, Authoritarian Computer Voice." Splagner beckoned Graxnix over and activated the controls with over-exaggerated movements, making it more than obvious which ones were used. "Internal bay seals on. Air pumps to extract. Pressure dropping. Now zero. Activating bay door." Splagner wiggled a gloved tentacle across the console and the wall folded out to reveal the infinite deepness of space.

Graxnix inhaled deeply and stepped forward. They pointed their second lefty at a swirl of stars off to the bottom left of the space they could now see. Stars and galaxies whirled through the inky blackness, blazing with energy. It was sights like this that made it clear to Graxnix why prehistoric people thought the galaxies were gods, their tentacles reaching out across the heavens to control destinies.

Splagner walked up to join him. "Well majestic. It always gets me right in the centre of my valve assemblage."

The computer cut in, drowning out Splagner's satisfied sigh. "May I remind you that you are not here to stargaze but rather collect detritus. This lax attitude is most likely why you are here. Now, that item to the top right is a potential hazard to navigation and you should bring it in."

Splagner turned back to the console. "Hey, dude, you any good with a grab tentacle? It's just like those prize booths at the fair."

Graxnix shrugged, an action impossible to see through the space suit, and looked over the controls. "Looks easy enough." They rippled their tentacles over the controls and the robotic tentacle slowly extended out through the hatchway.

Splagner slapped Graxnix on their back. "Hey, you're a natural, Graxy. Think you can grab that thing out there?"

"Of course." Graxnix manipulated the controls and soon enough had hold of the object. It was roughly oblong and the robotic tentacle had clamped onto it at one end. As Graxnix retracted the arm the object began to twist. "Hey, what's going on? Something is pulling the tentacle off its axis."

"You have not compensated for the artificial gravity edge effects. Kindly do so." If anything, Graxnix felt that the computer voice had got louder, which made the change to Splagner even more difficult.

"Hey there, Graxy, watch for the fringing. The ship's artificial gravity is working right out to the edge of that bay door and as you get closer it's working on the garbage too. Bring it in slowly and so it'll land softly on the bay floor."

Graxnix worked to counter the pull of the artificial gravity, twisting the tentacle and eventually, with a thump, delivering the garbage onto the extended bay door. "Splagner, that's nothing like those prize booths at the fair. There you just drop it from the sucker into a chute."

Splagner raised their upper tentacles in an exaggerated shrug that could be seen in a space suit. "Sucker's don't work in a vacuum, but it's close enough. Let's see what you've pulled in." Showing more enthusiasm than at any point since Graxnix had met them, but still not a huge amount, Splagner flowed over to the object. "Wow, would you look at this weird-looking thing. It's like an old ground car that's been made by someone who's never seen one before."

"An astute observation, Splagner Gardont." The computer's voice was now quieter. To Graxnix it sounded interested, rather than its usual angry timbre. "It does bear similarities to primitive ground transport from several cultures. Early enough to require wheels."

Graxnix walked along the object. It was larger than any ground car they'd seen, although it did follow the basic shape. Not as aerodynamic as their parents' one and looking really strange where the wheels broke through the bodywork to touch the floor. The wheels were metallic and looked very poor for gripping any surface. They, along with the main bodywork, were badly pocked and scarred from micrometeorite collisions but it looked to Graxnix like there might have been some black covering on the wheels at some point. Looking at the body he saw that this was also metallic and had possibly had a red colouring. About midway along was what might have once been a clear screen on the front of a cabin. Graxnix walked up to it and peered in through the cracked and starred screen. "Hey, is this an alien in here? Some weird, four-limbed one?"

"Negative, there are organic compounds present inside that may once have made up an occupant but they have long decomposed."

"Wow, so there was like a pilot, maybe?"

"No significant mechanics or electronics are detected in there either. It appears to be only a primitive vacuum suit with insufficient life-support facilities. If this had been a pilot they would not have survived for long." The computer's voice was still quiet, the hint of interest continuing. Graxnix looked back to Splagner, who appeared to have lost interest in the object and was watching the stars. They turned back to look inside the cabin again.

"So more likely a burial ritual or something? Wasteful, but plenty of cultures we've looked at on my course would do similarly strange and wasteful things in the name of religion, if not so advanced." Graxnix peered further inside. "There looks to be some markings here." They wiped at a panel. Once the dust was cleared a design was revealed that meant nothing to Graxnix but looked a bit like this:

DON'T PANIC

"Computer, can you translate this?"

The computer's voice rose in volume once again. "I am not a translation device and even if I were, there is not enough there to even begin. I now understand why my fellow AIs complain if they're sent to accompany archaeological expeditions, if this is the level of request they receive."

"Ok, ok, was just asking. I was simply thinking that if someone was going to fire an old ground car into space they'd have left a message on it to tell the gods or whoever found it who the body was. Some great king or similar, perhaps."

A burbling chuckle rolled out of the suit speakers as Splagner bent over and slapped their third lefty with their second. "Good one, Graxy. As if anyone with enough technology to collect this heap of ancient junk would even bother to translate a message.

Who cares what a species who've only just climbed out of the oceans has to say."

Graxnix paused for a moment, offended and appalled. They might have had misgivings about studying archaeology and ancient history at university but if they managed to get through this community service with a good report Graxnix hoped to continue with their studies and so took Splagner's insult personally. Archaeology was as valid a field of research as any other – indeed, as civilisation expanded and ruins of other long dead civilisations

were found, it was essential to understanding, and avoiding, how those civilisations died. Graxnix had heard a lecturer say that in his first term but now, faced with his find, he finally understood it. "This could be a vitally important find, leading to  a previously unknown species and even, possibly, a first contact situation. Computer, surely there are procedures for this sort of thing?"

"I am afraid you are labouring under a misapprehension, Graxnix Pindom, that this is a deep space naval exploration vehicle. This is a garbage recovery vehicle operated by the Ridnor Community Council and I can assure you that the council has neither the interest nor the funds for anything as esoteric as new civilisations. This garbage will be taken back to Ridnor, broken apart to recover the trace amounts of precious elements, and the rest then sold for scrap. That might, just, cover the cost that you have placed on society by requiring criminal punishment."

"You can't be serious. Look, someone fired this into space. There are messages on it that could help us understand why." They pointed at the DON'T PANIC design and then moved to the back to point to a second design, under a patina of micro-meteorite craters and interstellar dust;

TESLA

"They should be translated. This should go to the university. There are people in the archaeology department who would be fascinated by this. There could be a civilisation out there right now waiting for a response. Imagine them waiting for years, hoping to someday meet another civilisation and we just ignore it. That would be terrible."

"That is of no interest to me and should not be to you, Graxnix Pindom. All that should be of interest to you is doing as I command to get a good report. There are thousands of worlds out there right now at a level to throw this sort of junk into space and there is nothing worth learning from them until they can at least propel a living specimen outside of their own system. As, statistically, most civilisations do not get beyond early space travel before destroying themselves it is not financially viable to investigate all items of this type."

Graxnix slumped inside their space suit. They hadn't thought they were that bothered by what they were doing at university, only going because their parents had insisted, but the thought of this artefact from a primitive civilisation being lost to science actively made Graxnix sad. It would seem they really did care. But the computer was right, they weren't going to be able to do anything about it unless they got a good report on their community service and got back to their studies.

"OK, I see where this is going. I'll shut up now."

"Very good." The computer voice from the suit speakers raised in volume. "Splagner Gardont, stop staring at the stars and close the bay doors. We are finished here. The two of you will report to the bridge to run a manual scan of the area for further detritus. I shall store this garbage."

Splagner turned away from the view and walked over to the console, where they closed the door and repressurised the bay. After removing their suits Splagner left and Graxnix stopped at the door to look back at the strange-looking ground car. All pockmarked from micrometeorites and yet shiny with possibilities. Graxnix would talk to their professor when they got back to university about this and see if there was any way to get hold of the car, and any other items like it, that the garbage collectors found. No matter how poor the statistics were, the people Graxnix imagined waiting for their response should not be ignored. Graxnix was shaken out of their reverie by the computer's voice once more.

"You are dawdling, Graxnix Pindom, that will not encourage me to produce a good report." The robot tentacle picked up the object and flicked it into the back of the garbage bay and onto the pile of assorted items, mostly rocks but with the odd machined thing, where it landed with a crunch that made Graxnix wince. "I'm still waiting, Graxnix Pindom."

Graxnix sighed, resolved once more to do something about this waste of precious archaeology, and made their way to the control room.

Brian M. Milton lives on the outskirts of Glasgow, where he spends his out of work time dodging bees and cows while trying to think of silly stories. He is a member of the Glasgow Science Fiction Writers' Circle and has all the bruises from their 'robust' critiques to prove it.
He has previously been published in markets such as *Fireside Fiction* and *KZine* for both SF and fantasy but this is the first time he's written about delinquent interstellar starfish.
Brian can often be found jabbering on the Twitters @munchkinstein

Take a bunch of science fiction writers, a cluster of astronomers and a pair of artists, and throw them into a room. Give them a whiteboard, a pile of sandwiches and a pot of coffee. Let's see what happens.

Simon Malpas and Deborah Scott of Edinburgh University did just that: the result is this collection of stories, essays and artwork, *Scotland in Space: Creative Visions and Critical Reflections on Scotland's Space Futures*

Scotland in Space, with stories from Laura Lam, Russell Jones and Pippa Goldschmidt, and with a foreword by Ken MacLeod is published by *Shoreline of Infinity*.

It is available as a full colour paperback from the website and in all good bookshops.

www.shorelineofinfinity.com

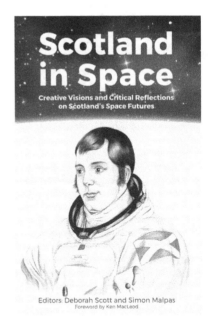

Editors: Deborah Scott and Simon Malpas
Foreword by Ken MacLeod

"*Scotland in Space* refreshingly captures the many contributions in scientific, science-fictional and artistic studies from one of the world's top three per capita contributors to astronomy and space research – another welcome indicator that small is beautiful against the current Mega-power trends."
— The late John Campbell Brown, Astronomer Royal for Scotland

"*Scotland in Space* is by turns enlightening and entertaining."
— Eric Brown, The Guardian,

Galaxies of Rotten Stars

dave ring

It should have been a night of celebration.

"Champagne for the toast, your tremendousness?"

The server's face bore a nervous obsequity that couldn't be more grating. I drained a glass of champagne and returned it to her tray before she could walk away. An alcohol-induced flush traveled from my chest to my cheeks. I loosened the red tie at my neck, absentmindedly flicking away the bit of Scotch Tape that had held the little end in place.

It was 11:58pm. I met the eyes of my advisor, Kelline, across the crowded room. She looked down at her watch, a sleek band of silver that encircled her slim forearm. The room could have buckled under the weight of the power and wealth contained in the suited men and gowned women within, but, for a minute, it was as if there were nothing but myself and Kelline's implacable expression. At exactly 11:59:31, she looked up from her watch and started counting down – "Thirty, twenty-nine, twenty-eight..." – and as the room took up the chant, I could hear the off-kilter echo of the real time being shouted from the crowds outside the manor. The hot friction of the miscount filled me with a low drip of power, like a growing static charge, until I was buzzing. My dessicated dick twitched in my shorts, trying valiantly to get hard. I abandoned the party for the kitchen. As I touched the pantry door, the power left me like a orgasm.

The door opened to a wretched stairwell instead of rows of carefully stacked canned food and dry goods. I entered the stairwell, panting, and left the cheers of the new year for a humid darkness filled with dank debris. The light from the pantry cut through the dust of the stairwell like an unwelcome knife, exposing ugly innards meant to be hidden. Refuse littered the ground. Gaps in the ceiling tiles exposed rotten beams, each bearing a haphazard collection of mildew and sludge.

The pantry door slammed shut and everything was dark once more. I took a deep breath that caught in my lungs. I hacked and coughed, my retching the only noise in the wet darkness. It wasn't just the air. Time here was strange and sticky. I could spend a week on the landing and only a few seconds would have passed at home. I crept cautiously through the mire with a series of noisome steps, mindless of the fungal colonies I was crushing and rendering into further dust. I hadn't gone two steps before my right hip socket was a throbbing knot, the ache a reminder of my purpose. I needed to fill the well of my power.

My hand found the railing from memory, but recoiled as it met wrought iron dripping with condensation. When I'd first made this place, I hadn't counted on the toll that uneven time would take on it. The narrow beam of the flashlight I'd brought with me shone on smaller segments of decay framed by comforting darkness, like looking through a keyhole.

The oval of light swept sideways until it framed a face, one I would have recognized in my mirror three or four decades ago. The face grimaced at me, blinking in the sudden light. I drew the light downwards, to where the flesh of its neck became a torn tapestry of skin that exposed the inner workings of its chassis. Mangled pipe veins and a rusted motherboard dangled from the iron spine that protruded from its torso. It hung suspended from a harness attached to the wagon that halfway juts through the hole it made in the wall. Some of the writing was still visible on the paneling:

DI TR CT ISTIL ING.

I'd driven that wagon through the wall myself. This scrap of reality had barely a thousand square feet to it, and the wagon could have been an awning or an alchemy set. Anything. It was all just symbols, but symbols were enough for the animus. They gave the power something to cling to, made it volatile, and the impossibility of this space that should exist, linked to this particular prisoner, then became the heat, the transfer of energy.

Something rustled above me as I regarded the ruined not-man and I flinched. Nothing in that place should have had life but the fungus and the sorry construct. I turned away from it and pointed the flashlight towards the stairs. Nothing moved.

"You're back," it said with my voice. I returned the flashlight to its mangled face and frowned. It usually didn't like to speak to me. I felt the same. My bladder ached uncomfortably—the champagne had coursed through my body quickly. I grunted and unzipped my fly. The light sparkled on the arc of urine between my body and its ruptured torso. It said nothing as piss puddled beneath it.

The degradation wasn't necessary; our proximity alone filled me with animus. The animus was a steadier power than that earned through manipulating the friction of time. More stable. Galaxies were nurtured in my metaphysical gut. Constellations of power that pulsed and seethed, bubbling in my esophagus. As if on a warm updraft, a star might rise up and crash against the curtain of my teeth before falling back into the cauldron of animus from where they'd come.

There, again—that rustling. It was unmistakably a visitor in a place that should have none. I shook the last remaining urine from my prick and zipped my fly, scanning the stairwell with light. My hip no longer ached; the animus restored more than just my power. What did I care about an intruder, no matter the strangeness of it? Who could touch me?

"You are swine," the not-man said with my voice. It was trying to distract me. I back-handed it without thinking. A ring on my finger caught and tore at a loose flap of its skin, exposing the circuitry along its cheekbone. I shook off the shred of synthetic flesh as if it were a cobweb.

"Better swine than less than a man," I said. Power crackled in me. I could entertain some small insolence in exchange for feeling so full of life. It was time to leave. "Until next time, you—"

My farewell was interrupted by a fist that wedged itself into my open mouth.

The blow rocked me back. My jaw ached and swelled while I tried in vain to pronounce words of power, but the galaxies couldn't be unleashed. My tongue flicked against hard knuckle. Another of my attacker's fists collided with my gut. I fell to my knees in the still-warm puddle of urine, the assailant pushing me to the ground. I wheezed helplessly through my nose.

I clawed at their arm but they were unmoved, though my nails grew slick with their blood. The keyhole of light pointed at my assailant's shoes. Some kind of strange leather, thick and articulated like crocodile hide. Their fist struck my gut again and again. While the breath was knocked out of me, unable still to speak them into oblivion, I found myself flipped over on my back. My assailant removed their fist from my mouth and lowered their face to mine.

Was it a kiss or something else? A wave of unsolicited desire went through me as their tongue forced its way into my mouth. Even while my animus-repaired erection became uncomfortable in the crush between our bodies, I realized that my assailant's purpose was far more intimate than it seemed. Their kiss drew the animus from me as with a syringe; they left me with vacuum. Excitement fled my loins, leaving behind a slime-like smear.

When they got to their feet, my well dry, I felt the absence of them like Melanija departing from our bed in the cold light of morning.

"I told you he'd be here," said the not-man, with my face, with my voice.

"I should have listened to you sooner," my assailant said, and a buzzing shock emanated from the base of my neck. They *too* had my voice. They picked up my flashlight and pointed it towards the not-man.

"Don't leave me like this. Not with him," the not-man said.

"You'd die in my world." Did my assailant sound different, with the animus coursing through them?

"I don't think you truly have a sense of how long I've been here," the not-man said. "I don't want to go with you. I know what I'm asking. This is the twenty-third time he has come here."

I tried to speak. "Who are—"

"Twenty-third," my assailant repeated, interrupting me. "Every one of his new years, he visits, you said. That's—"

"More than ten thousand years between visits," the not-man said without affectation.

"And he's a bad man, you said? Truly?"

Though my hair was wet with my own piss, and my belly cavernous with the absence of animus, I couldn't help but speak again. "Neither of you are fit to clean the shit from my chamberpot," I spat out.

My assailant kicked me. A rib snapped.

"So many of us are bad men," they said. "In so many worlds. It is an unceasing warning that I will do my best to not lose sight of."

So pretentious. But beneath the pain, beneath the indignity, I felt a new star being born in me. It was slow, and the star was small; the presence of my attacker must be impeding the process. Were we so alike that it confused the distillation? But it would be enough to unmake that stairwell between worlds, and disgorge us all to our own times. I only needed another moment. I moaned, a melange of pain and pleasure.

The not-man's gaze, still caught in that keyhole of light, flicked at me with a discernment I hadn't reckoned with.

"That leech must be ended," it said.

My assailant held the flashlight beneath their chin with one hand, like a child preparing to tell a ghost story. A jaw I hadn't seen since my twenties looked back at me. There were small signs of refraction, differences between my choices and whatever life they'd lived in the infinite array of possible worlds: the lurid orange of their skin, the rugged beard of their cheeks, the silver ring that punctured the quivering supercilious sphincter of their mouth. The animus was rejuvenating *them* now; there was already a shock of sandy brown hair running through their gray mane like a seam of gold.

"I want you to watch me crush your only chance of escape," they said, from within the now distorted keyhole. Their free hand darted through the darkness. Steam hissed from a severed alchemical boiler in the not-man's chassis. The star died in my chest, and with it, my pride.

"Send me back." I got slowly to my sore knees, soaking my shins. "You have everything. Just send me back." I felt like nothing without the animus, just a slab of dying skin, but I was still powerful in my world. Still king.

My assailant brought me to my feet and held me close, ignoring the sodden state of me, their body flexing with a muscularity that I'd long since lost. "How often did you visit him?" they asked. The bass of their voice rumbled between our bodies.

"Every year," I said, desperation unfurling in my throat. I clutched at them with ineffective hands, settling around their waist like a prom date. I would have fallen if they'd let me go.

"Once a year," they said, like it settled something. Their breath was warm against my cheek.

I let hope grow a seed in me. I could endure anything if it meant going home. I turned my head and exhaled, looking up at their face. At our face. When their mouth met mine, I focused on the stubble on their jaw and parted my lips. It was a skilled kiss, a strong kiss. I didn't even notice when their tongue tied a hex in my mouth like a cherry stem, until something between us changed. An inchoate sea change began eroding my edges, killing that fragile hope. I was no longer the vessel being filled with animus – I was the still. A screeching filled the stairwell. I couldn't recognize it as my own desperation even as the sound of it burned in my throat.

The not-man's chassis crashed to the ground when they unlatched it from the harness. They had to hoist me up, still screaming, to get the leather straps around my shoulders. My feet flailed helplessly; I could only touch the ground if I pointed my toes downward like a ballerina. I blinked at them as they studied me, blinded by the narrow ray of the flashlight.

They spoke words of power I almost recognized. Envy bloomed in me at the sound; those syllables should be hatching in my mouth, not theirs. A string of drool fell from my sagging lip. They opened the emergency exit. Instead of revealing a cramped access tunnel, daylight flooded the room. I averted my eyes from the not-man's discarded hull and tried to meet the eyes of my undoing with something approaching pride. Behind them, on the other side of the door, there was a white house, gleaming and columned, surrounded by red and cream tulips. Something was eerily familiar about it. If I squinted, I could almost imagine my manor on that lawn, grey and sprawling, adorned with turrets instead of tulips.

"We are terrible men, Donal. Truly terrible." They stepped through, looking over their shoulder. "I'll be back in a year. Spend the time wisely."

The door swung shut between us. The screaming had started again. Would Melanija miss me in the morning? Would Kelline be disappointed? Or would they both rise up to take my place? Through all my questions, amidst my own blistering wailing, the afterimage of that white house hung against my eyelids like a mirage.

---

dave ring is the chair of the OutWrite LGBTQ Book Festival in Washington, DC. He is the publisher of Neon Hemlock Press as well as the editor of *Broken Metropolis: Queer Tales of a City That Never Was* from Mason Jar Press. More info at www.dave-ring.com.

Goatherd Inquisition

Jeremy Nelson

'd never seen anyone with so much tattooed computation. The inquisitor's skin, from eyelids to bare scalp to the ends of their fingers, was traced and dotted with circuitry. They did not take the seat I offered. Instead, they loomed over the cheese.

Understandable, I thought. Most people did not have the opportunity to see a whole wheel in the flesh. Under the rind's filigree, its rounded sides were black with *percissice tienoticus*. The cheese's surface, roughened to a tree-bark texture, indicated the interior had matured to an ideal liver-like consistency.

As liaison, introductions were my obligation. I gestured to the man on the other side of the table. "May I present Citizen Xiemin. Pride of the Moon, his dairy is recognized as Superlative in its quality and consistency."

The goatherd sat serene in the pooled fabric of his robes. He nodded in acknowledgment.

Silent all through their arrival in our produce terminal, the inquisitor at last deigned to speak. "This cheese is a representative sample?"

"Yes, inquisitor sir." The goatherd's voice rasped in the crisp terminal air. "The wheel nears maturity. Considering its brethren, the wheel ought to be exquisite."

"Gastronomy is not the root of our concern. I've been sent to investigate anomalous reports of *life* from your moon's exports."

Art: Siobhan McDonald   53

I kept myself from offering an answer. Who better to speak on the nature of cheese than a goatherd?

"Yes, all good cheese is a thing of life. A symphonic work of microbiota and milk."

But sporadic clarifications wouldn't hurt. "Specifically, milk of the wek-goat. Our herd is of impeccable breeding. Best of the Arc."

"I do not," the inquisitor said, "merely refer to fermentation necessary to congeal protein. I speak of the troubling claim that your cheese ascends to a more sophisticated state of being." He projected some of our more attention-grabbing advertising materials on the wall: Thonxus Cheese, swaddled like an infant and being shared in thin slices by a smiling Earth family. The text was legible behind the cheese's rising fumes. *"Eating... a transcendent form of connection."*

The goatherd didn't seem inclined to reply. No one respectable would sully themselves commenting on Tourist Bureau work. The scent settled in the room and into my pores. I did my best to relax into the smothering odour. It was impressive that the inquisitor seemed so unaffected. Perhaps cybernetic senses allowed them to disregard stimuli.

"Citizens," they said. "I establish fact, then act accordingly. Should anecdotal accounts prove to be untrue, then my work is done. If new truths are uncovered, my visit is documented, and my work is done. Consequences are dealt in proportion to the hindrance of an inquisition."

I broke the silence that followed. "It's our absolute intention and privilege to assist."

"The cheese is near fully mature," said the goatherd. "Your questions will be addressed."

Goatherd Xiemin had such timing, truly the best of his generation. Even as he finished speaking, the cheese gave a characteristic *bur-r-rap*, as the air trapped at the top of the wheel finally split its skin and escaped – exposing the cheese's interior to the open air.

There was a definite moist character to the atmosphere now. But the inquisitor did not waver. "Is this marketing hyperbole? The sensual experience is such that it takes on a life of its own?"

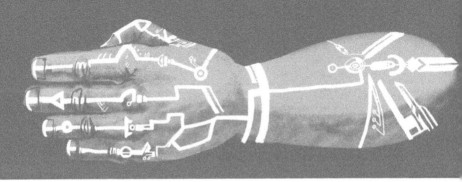

"Give it time, sir inquisitor." The goatherd kept his gaze on the cheese. I didn't blame him. These moments were special.

The split membrane vibrated, just enough to blur it to the eye. And the room was filled with not just scent but sound. A resonance of artisanal quality at 415Hz.

"Singing's begun," said the goatherd.

"Is that all?" I could almost see computations feed into the inquisitor's optics as they spoke. "Microbiota interact with trapped air to generate turbulence enough to maintain a pitch. Should the microbes be acting in unison, the specimen would still be no more complex than a siphonophore—"

Their words faltered, though, as the cheese not only continued to sing but pulsed its notes in time with their words. "This is noteworthy," was all they said.

"It'd be a shame, putting cheese at its prime to waste," said the goatherd. He pulled out a cheese set from somewhere in his loose-fitting robes. To preserve freshness, the clean cuts of a viceknife was preferred.

"And if the cheese continues to mature?"

"After an orbit and a half, it deteriorates. The membrane sloughs off, and what's left is very tough to handle."

"Tough?"

"Practically lethal to humans. Too good to let it go to waste like that."

The blade was keen and no wider than my thumb. The vice ringed neatly around the wheel, the mounted blade swinging free to cut fine wedges from the block.

And just in time. Pulsating song had turned into something more familiar. The vibrating membrane fumbled with syllables. *Ta. Da. Ta ba la. Li le lieeeeh...*

"Hypnotic," said the goatherd. "Isn't it?"

The inquisitor, perhaps for the first time, seemed interested. "What prompts such vocalizations?"

"It's got new equipment to work with," said the goatherd, gesturing at the split membrane with his eyebrows while his hands held the knife level. "I expect most of the learning happens during aging."

Heel-uh.

The inquisitor, in their gravest voice, said "This is not known to Science."

"It does make the cheese taste better."

"Oh yes," I said.

Hel-oh, it stuttered as the first cut was made from its center to the outer rind. *Hello-oh?* The other cut was just a knuckle further on the arc. With the viceknife the goatherd levered the narrow slice from the round. The cheese shone translucent pearl, marbled green throughout. At its top, rind rose from flesh, separated but for countless threads stretching from cheese to domed membrane. Smaller knives split the captive slice into more manageable portions.

"We export these slices, frozen, for those who cannot afford to bring a wheel to maturation. Uncut cheese cannot be kept in shipping indefinitely; too ripe and they're inedible, refrigerated too long and they never voice."

The goatherd laid a film-thin slice of cheese over a crispbread disc – had that also been in his pockets? – and offered it to the inquisitor with seasoned words.

"Is the cheese not alive? Is it not bred to be eaten? In our farms, there is no great mystery to be found."

The inquisitor took the bread and ate the cheese. Foreign or not, I knew a happy customer when I saw one.

Jeremy Nelson is a recent transplant to Edinburgh whose afterimages linger in Hong Kong and Portland, Oregon. His preoccupations include accordions, photography, and outdated methods of putting words to paper. He holds an MFA from Vermont College of Fine Arts.

SCOTLAND'S FESTIVAL OF SCIENCE FICTION, FANTASY & HORROR WRITING

BACK FOR A SECOND YEAR

Meet local, national and international authors

Test your knowledge on our quiz

Entertain us with your work at our open mic

Submit to our writing competition

Dance the night away at our ceilidh

Feast your eyes on the works and publications
in our creators' hall

Relish in the thrills of a Shoreline of Infinity's
Event Horizon

Friday 5th June 2020 – Sunday 7th June

The Pleasance, Edinburgh

Full details, programme and tickets:

www.cymerafestival.co.uk

Twitter: @CymeraF

Ultimate code

Peyman Saremian

We see them as dots in three colors; red, yellow and green. We can guess their next move. We can see everything that crosses their minds. We are the guests of their minds, even though they don't notice us.

I was bored. I had no tension dot; all of them were green. It was good news but I wasn't happy. I needed a challenge, something that didn't exist for me in this concrete building. The other employees peered into their small monitors, controlling the behaviour of their dots.

Yesterday, the most exciting thought that I blocked from the mind of a dot was this: why must I pay for my stepdaughter's expenses? Last week, one dot was thinking about choking the neighbour's dog for barking the whole night. And the last month, a dot thought about the origin of cats and where they came from. These were the most noticeable cases that I could be proud of blocking; the yellow dots.

I drank my breakfast coffee quickly. It was hot, but felt good. I was pleased with myself for not waiting for it to cool down like other people. The green dots, the green dots … damn these green dots. Perhaps because I was new, they gave me this area where the people's thoughts had been accommodating our codes over several years, and their minds had become conservative and prudent.

But while I was throwing the cup into the rubbish bin under my desk, I saw it. There it was, my red dot, my first red dot.

Upper-level employees had been detecting the red dots for years. They were no different to yellow or green for them, but it was a great discovery for me and made my heart pound like crazy. I had to open the dot, read its mind map and block the negative thoughts in the shortest possible time, and finally report it to my senior management.

"I want to kill myself. I want to be free."

Oh my God, a suicide case! I opened it, assuming it would be a thought about assassinating the president or doubting the whole system. But the description of the thought showed that it was just a suicide. A thought that had crossed the red line; it was a great start for me. It wasn't moving, it was just developing the suicide idea and thinking about ending its life. We never had any information about where the dots lived or what gender they were. They were just intelligent dots that had to be under control. I clicked on the dot and its name appeared on my screen, DK 101077.

With some simple code that I typed, I removed the suicide idea from its mind forever. Sometimes a guardian angel does his work behind a desk.

It was my first red dot. I appreciated it for having such a thought. Now I wasn't that amateur, inexperienced employee. They should apply the label to someone else. I hoped the red dots would start flowing to me and get me promoted.

"No, don't be stupid. Nobody is controlling us. Why? Because you can think about everything you want right now. Come on, think about a nuclear bomb, can't you? Ok, everything's good? All right, get back to work."

We always had such discussions with the new ones; we, the experienced employees. After two years working here, now I was a member of an elders' club; a man who had turned several reds into green. Now I was the manager of my own section on the floor. I only dealt with those reds that operators didn't know how to manage without hurting the dot's brain.

I should have been happy, but I wasn't. My screen monitor was empty in those days, no dot, no map. It meant I had no influence on anyone's life anymore. I had been peering into the empty screen for weeks, till my lucky day arrived. The big red dot, my beautiful big red dot.

I put on my glasses, then laid my hands on the keyboard like a professional piano player. "Let's see what we have. Oh, something bad is here." I opened its mind map.

"Am I the only one who can hear the voices?"

"What does that mean? Our voices? Or its delusional voices?"

"I should write it down."

"Writing?! Ok, beautiful big red. Goodbye." But suddenly its name caught my eye: DK 101077.

"Oh, my God! Is that you? It's been a while, my old friend. But sorry, I should turn you. Or should I?"

If I made it green, I wouldn't have any red dots for a long time. Besides, it was my old friend: my first red dot. My finger remained floating in the air; apparently the piano player had forgotten his note.

For almost two months, DK wrote down everything that crossed its mind. And I was its only reader. It wrote about everything, ranging from the morning dew on a flower petal to doubting the existence of aliens. Its ideas were not so organised at first, but got better when it became more experienced at writing.

First, I promised myself that I would turn it when a new red came to me. But when the red dots filled my screen like raindrops; saving my own dot was the only thought I had.

"Can you hear me, God?"

"I'm not your god, DK."

"Why am I so different from everyone else?"

"Ok, ok. This game is over."

"Do I have a particular responsibility on my shoulders?"

"You're made of irresponsibility."

Now or never. I typed some simple code. It could end all its strange thoughts. And when it read its notes, it would find them meaningless.

"I want to write a book; a book about everything I imagine. Please help me."

Was I weak? Was I too kind? Or did I really want to read its book?

"I know you as a guardian angel. You don't belong to this world. You chose me, so I dedicate this book to you. It's not a book like every others. It's not about being passive and just living your life. It's about things that I'm feeling. Things that exist but nobody sees them. It's a story of a world that I can't see in other people's minds, the world of…"

I let it use *imagination*.

"… imagination."

Why I couldn't stop it? Did somebody prevent me? Was somebody reading my mind? I had to stop it; it had gone too far. Hearing its thoughts was a harmful addiction. I shouldn't have been a victim of its imagination. Now I needed more complicated codes to turn it, which may cause brain damage, even though I didn't want to use them. So it may die because of my irresponsibility.

It finished the first book very soon; it spent many days thinking about this book with its inchoate imagination. I liked its work. If it had sat in front of me, I would have encouraged it for hours. It was seeing the world in a pure and innocent way.

"I should give my book to a friend to see what other people think about it."

"No, no, my DK. I read it; it's perfect. Please, no."

"I wish the whole world understood what I'm thinking."

"Damn, DK. Don't put me in this situation."

"Maybe there are other people like me. I should find them."

That's it.

After a six-month one-sided friendship with DK, I had to say goodbye with a few code lines.

"I…"

Enter.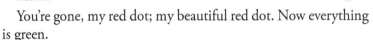

You're gone, my red dot; my beautiful red dot. Now everything is green.

"No, nobody is controlling us. You can think whatever you want. Think about destroying the Earth right now. You see? Nobody is controlling you. You've been chosen from the people. You're lucky. Understand?" The manager of a small section was talking excitedly with the new ones. After this many years, I still sometimes went to the refectories on the lower floors. Such discussions were interesting to me. Now my office was on the top floor, below the general manager's floor. Nobody knew exactly what the general manager's duties were. He worked on cases beyond other people's abilities.

I didn't deal with the dots anymore; I was destroying the patterns now. A pattern consisted of a lot of big red dots following the same line of thought and with a similar mentality. I was working on a pattern that I named the 'butterfly pattern' because of the way it looked. It took months to write code just to visualise the butterfly. Then I would send the code to the lower floors so they could turn the dots one by one.

The writing process of my complicated code was nearly finished. I had worked for months on it. When the day came, I said goodbye to the big butterfly. It lost its wings first and then its body broke apart into a thousand dots. I leaned back, happy with the result. But something impossible happened. After a few minutes, the dots attached together again. I ran the code one more time but it was pointless. My efforts ended with complete failure. Which part of my code was wrong? I had destroyed more complicated patterns before. Apparently I was dealing with difficult opponents; it was a good challenge for me. I had to write the best code of my life, a code that would make me proud for the rest of my life. I think it was on the eighth day that I found the answer with a code that could duplicate itself for an infinite time. There was no way for any butterfly to survive.

"Hey butterfly, you're ready to say goodbye?"

Suddenly a dot from the head of the butterfly detached itself and went to the corner of the screen. I hadn't run my code yet, so that couldn't have been the reason. Somehow it seemed to break its mental connection with the others, or maybe it had detected what I was going to do. In a strange way, I felt familiar with it. So I clicked and opened its map.

DK 101077.

"Of course it's you."

I wasn't an emotional person; I never have been. But my eyes got wet and my hands started to shake when I saw its name.

"I'm glad to see you're alive. But you've gone too far. You're a member of a pattern now."

"I know you're supporting me."

"It wasn't the case last time."

"I have a big responsibility on my shoulders."

"It's all my fault. I let you get in trouble."

"You're my guardian."

"No, I'm not."

"You have a responsibility too."

"Wait a minute. You can hear me?!"

A note appeared on the screen: *I can feel you.*

I was shocked.

"You've been my guardian in the worst of times."

"I can run the code right now. I can destroy all of you; I have this power."

"You are different from others."

"No, I'm not."

"You were the starter."

"Now I'm your finisher."

But I couldn't run the code. What was preventing me? The red dot went back to the head of the butterfly. Were they controlling my mind or was I controlling theirs? Did they have so much power now? If united minds could make such a beautiful pattern, why would I destroy it? The doubts took over me.

I neither destroyed the butterfly, nor let it go. I could make a decision. I was in control of my mind. Or was I?

This butterfly had come a long way. It needed one more step to fly; yeah, one step, one floor.

"I'll put your destiny in the general manager's hands. Goodbye, beautiful butterfly. I hope you always fly in the sky of imagination."

I sent the special case to the general manager.

I hoped he had doubts too.

Born in 1985 in Iran, **Peyman Saremian** is an animator, graphist, short film maker and a writer. He mostly writes science fiction and fantasy, loves to imagine alternative universes and challenge reality. If his characters let him get away, he works on his scripts and short films too. He's currently working on his first novel.

The Overwrite

Raymond W Gallacher

They told me there were eighty thousand people in New Talinn. Or at least they would be recognisable as people. The overfly never really tells us much. We record, collate and analyse a flood of information, from road traffic to peak data use. It produces indicators, nothing more. The pivots don't confirm anything. The behaviours of human populations are a thing of such complex nuance that no number set can capture it. But in New Talinn, some indicators were suspicious: a drop in communication with other colonies, a tailing off in external trade, no further intake of new skilled workers or agricultural ones. It was suggestive of a city drawing in on itself. It was suspicious enough for us to put a cordon around the city and then look for a way in.

But we knew. Another city fallen. Eighty thousand souls.

"What was the excuse?"

"Unusually violent local weather," Gleniffer said. "It's as good a reason for our presence as any." He caressed the cross around his neck. He did that a lot. Once I thought it was a nervous reaction, but John Gleniffer was not a nervous man. Our relationship had developed a lot since Castile. We had developed an understanding of each other's capabilities, if not trust.

"You need anything?"

"Nothing."

"You certainly look the part. Matching clothes, sympathetic style. They did a good job."

"It wasn't hard. It's an agricultural community, mainly. There's augmentation but very little interest in high style or physical change."

"No wings needed?"

He smiled. I didn't always catch his joke questions. "No, I don't need wings. Not today."

I touched the thin metal lace that grew back from my temple. It was still uncomfortable to wear. The augment was fake, of course. There was no nano penetration underneath it, but it looked like what everyone else in the city would be wearing. My differentness should not be detectable. Not at first.

New Talinn was just a reconnaissance job. Warrant Officer Fordyce called it, "A quick in and an even quicker out."

That was my intention. I wouldn't give the city the chance to turn on me. We lost someone before. The people did it with their bare hands. That was unthinkable, the closeness, the intimacy of that. I didn't linger on it.

"Fordyce's breaching party have found a good spot outside the weather shielding. There nothing but a park on the other side of the wall. Then it's agricultural land and suburbs all the way to the city. We're thinking of breaching in about an hour's time, you'll just look like a late commuter. It's dark early here, Peter, so sit quietly and hide up if you see symptoms. If you have to run, it might be easier in the dark."

Symptoms. It was easier if we were medical about it.

"That okay with you, Peter?"

"Yes, sir."

"Glen's fine. We're hardly straight military." Gleniffer was in DF uniform, plain olive drab fatigues with few emblems apart from a golden loop on his shoulders. I always liked our uniforms. Now, I never wear one.

Gleniffer treated his command carrier like his home. He made it comfortable, with metal shelves full of little oddments that are his rather than the military's. He kept pictures of family, tiny pieces of artwork which were all childlike in style and a display of small crosses of stone or woven fibre. It makes others stare or laugh, especially Fordyce, but I can't see that it does any harm. It puts something human among the community of camouflaged military vehicles trying to melt into the prairie. And, as he said, we're hardly straight military. He reached back to a locker and took out a bottle of whisky. "Take one. Settle the nerves."

I liked taking a drink with him. He was undemanding. We could both sit in complete quiet. The hour before I go through the breach is one of my worst and best times. I tend not to talk and that makes others talk too much. The moments with Gleniffer were better. Outside the wind was whipping across the dry grass. I could hear it beat on the armoured walls of the carrier. Sometimes when it was strong enough, the carrier would rock back and forward on its tires. I liked that, even if it drove the other troops crazy.

"How long will it take for you to make an assessment?"

"Less than twelve hours. It doesn't take long. I meet people in the city, watch, talk, buy coffee, do ordinary things. I'll try and get to the Civic early if I can. Use the new toy."

Watching people is important. But what we need is a sample from Civic – that's the keystone. We can get a sample of the city's circulation from the barrier, but it's had no human interface. It doesn't help. I don't like that I have to get closer in to the city, but I hope it works.

The other way? I tried it. You find someone who is alone and follow them. When they go somewhere quiet, an alley, or even a restroom, you put a tranquilliser into them then tear at the augment on their head. You have to steady your hands enough to take a sample from the weeping blood and put it into a sealed container and get it back. It's too dangerous.

"We have permission for a full rewrite."

"Permission?"

"Okay, orders. If it's contaminated, what else can we do?"

We lapsed into silence. I like whisky, especially the peat essence in the better bottles. Gleniffer always has those. I enjoy the directness of the taste and scent. It's like being somewhere else, somewhere old and smoky and quiet, all log fires and dark wood.

"Do you think it's gone?" I asked.

"It doesn't look good. But I'll wait until you come back out. It's our own people, Peter. We have to be sure."

I had nothing to say and he took that for a question.

"If we knew how to get those people back, we would. In the here and now it's important that we get you back. Everything else? That's above my pay scale."

I believe that John Gleniffer likes me. To Gleniffer I am valuable because this will be my third time. I also know that he manages me. I'm an asset. They are frightened that I will be lost to them. Not just my own individuality, but that I will take everything I know with me.

He poured me another measure. That was just enough to wait out the time.

The breaching team was waiting for me near the city wall. Fordyce and his small team of specialists were kneeling down near the outer armour. It was only at a third of its full extension and still reached fifty metres above our heads. The alloy plates were pitted and scarred and looked beaten beyond their age. The settlers built a life in a tough place where the weather and meteor outbursts were worse than most: in their season, one is as destructive as the other.

I knelt down next to Fordyce. He was a good man. Like Gleniffer, he was quiet. The two near him I didn't recognise, they were just young, clean military faces. But Fordyce made good choices. He and his people would get me through in one piece and do everything they could to find me.

Fordyce had a cutter ring in his hand. His method was slick: create a few breaches in the same area so the ruptures look like meteor hits. The barrier repair process starts immediately and by that time, I'm through and his section has moved back to our screens. The city walls knew when they were being breached. An AI controlled city knows everything, in its way. They will learn to stop us at the outer wall, eventually. In time, machines learn. And then we're finished.

Sergeant Fordyce gripped my shoulder. "We'll cut a way back twenty meters from here. West. Find a way to mark it." He signalled with an open hand to my left. He tapped a timepiece on his fatigues. "Twelve or twenty-four?

I shook my head. "Six."

"We'll wait as long as we have to."

"Thanks."

There were six sharp, flat blasts then Fordyce and his men bundled me through before the city started to claw at itself.

On the other side I dropped onto soft moss on the floor of a small copse of trees. It couldn't have been better. When I got up, I walked carefully and slowly, looking straight ahead – just an unremarkable person. The secret is to be normal, really be that cardboard cut-out. Focus on the task and don't overthink.

I got out of the park and onto the road. I knew that there was a light monorail. Taking a ride would be taking a chance as there would be cameras and sensors in the cab and carriages, but it was the normal thing to do. I worried over the choice a little, but the monorail would save time and walking through farm land would draw more attention. I stood next to a stop sign, hands folded, face blank – a grey man. A blue and white train of carriages hissed down the rail and I took a moment to look around. The city was handsome, bio-block family homes sat back from the road with long yards of well-watered grass separating each house from its neighbour; and behind them were neat squares of farm land, some deep green, others turning to gold. It was church quiet and clean and tidy. No, it was more than clean, it was pristine. That's never a good sign. Still, some residential streets are just like a never-ending Sunday. What else would they be?

New Talinn wasn't hard to get around, all our cities were built on a similar pattern. That's what happens when your ancestors, fresh from cold sleep, need a city and don't have the time for high style. Permaculture parks and organised agriculture make up the outer rings. The greenery of high pines covers the ugliness of the barrier. Inward of the barrier, hamlets of small homes line roads and the roads make a spider web leading to the centre. The Civic area is grid-built and simple and is the canvas for all the things that humans do: spend their earnings, find someone to love, lose that love and regret what they've spent. All the benchmarks.

The Civic will have one more thing: the AI building. That stubby black tower supports and defends the city. It watches it, nurtures and heals it. It was the first thing to be powered when our forebears chose this prairie for a new home. Everything grows out from it. The hub of the wheel. It made the miracle of our life here.

I stepped onto the carriage and took my time. Every move I made was deliberate. It's best not to let your heartbeat rise, either through stress or through too much exertion. If you interact with a medical sensor it will arouse suspicion.

There were five of us in the carriage: three men, two women, and me. As far as I could see my clothing was right, or at least it was unremarkable. Everyone was calm, ordinary, one man idly checking the newsfeed above his head.

Once I'm in the shakes fade fast. Gleniffer made a good guess when he picked someone like me. When you don't interact well, you learn to keep your distance and to stay blank. That's why I've survived twice. I fit in. I'm good at grey.

I had been selected and inducted into the Defence Forces. The fitness training and tests were enjoyable for me. I prefer things that I can count rather than games. But still, I was out of place. There's always someone who looks for that.

Gleniffer came to see me after I had yet another day of disciplinary rock breaking. On his order I stood at ease in a dusty little office. "That's a bad scar," he said.

"It'll heal up."

"A fight?"

I thought of the farm boys back in the camp. "There's always someone who likes to fight."

"We don't use the best iron for nails."

"Sorry?"

"Old saying." Gleniffer looked out of the dusty windows onto the endless rows of makeshift huts. "The service doesn't always bring out the best in people." He picked up a pad and flicked through pages. "They're giving you a bad time. And reading between the lines, you're getting the worst of it and the blame." He tapped the pad. "Your enlistment could have been deferred."

I shook my head. "No, I've tried to rise beyond my... diagnosis."

I am an ordered person. Slightly on the spectrum, but I am aware of it and I manage myself and my relations with others.

It's not all bad. I'm good at being on my own, good at being individual. I can process and think things through. Most importantly, I don't overreact. Through a little less normality, I have become good at being normal.

He smiled. "Diagnosis? Wouldn't call it that. You're a little different. But you could be useful to me."

I found it wise to be silent. He would say what he needed to.

Gleniffer told me about the cities. About Gotland and St. Clair and the others, all changing and falling one after the other. About how he needed the right people, the kind of people who understood that humanity was losing in this colony. And could I be trusted not to talk about it?

That night I was invalided out of our pointless ground forces and found myself part of something else.

I stepped off the monorail into the centre of the city. People walked to work or looked in windows just like anywhere else, faces concentrated, sometimes chatting into their augment. Some people were with children, being frustrated at all the little things children do, maybe regretting their win on the pop-growth lottery. The kind of people you see every day.

I wasn't looking for them.

Amongst the crowds would be someone. This person would be my indicator, a flag amongst the everyday; nervous, afraid. Trying to understand a joke that they weren't in on. They guess they've lost their minds. Then that innocent, that uninfected will see something. An event so removed from normality that they know it is not at all a joke.

The sad thing is, I won't be able to do anything for them. Because I cannot be another outrider. I must not react the way they do. I must stay grey.

We don't know much. We know that the influence is not total. The city's AI is just doing what it has learned to do: to protect itself and us. We could never react quickly enough to the aggressive oddities of life on this planet. The meteor showers, the radiation flashes, the ocean storms. The city's armoured skin at the end of the AI's nerves have allowed us to flourish here. We grow, we make, we increase, and we thrive. We became fit for our world because we shielded ourselves from its excesses.

Not everyone would be linked. Children weren't but then it doesn't have to be one hundred per cent of the population for the city to be lost. That fact also would not alter the lethality of the cure.

I kept to public spaces, shopping areas and streets of cafés while I made my way inwards. Facial sensors were everywhere. It's problematic but that's public space: *"Something for tonight's supper. Step inside. See our specials."*

"Winter clothing starts here."

"Street trash is a criminal offence."

All that.

Given long enough I would be recognised as *other*. I would be found outside all the blockchains of data that maketh a man. Then, I would be on the run.

I had an idea that people were looking at me. It was hard to tell. Sometimes the job leads to paranoia. I slowed down and forced myself to be calm. Show nothing. Register nothing. If anything went wrong this close in to the city, I would never get back out. I took a sharp turn and went into a coffee shop. There was no smart plan to it, I just wanted to sit quietly and get grey again. Mostly, I just wanted some coffee. New Talinn has some of the best hydroponic beans on the colony and I wanted to take a moment and stare into the cup.

The coffee was excellent and the service mostly automated. Just what I wanted. Other people were there, at tables of their own, sipping and chatting quietly into their augment. It was a nice little place. My hand reached down towards my leg but I stopped the reaction and placed my hand deliberately on the table again. Nervous giveaways get detected if they are repeated.

I was armed with a nanophage stiletto. A normal firearm would have been detected and aroused the interest of the city patrol. It wasn't worth the effort. You can't fight an entire city. The best defence was to not get noticed. There were two newskin holsters on my thighs, both high up so that I could get to them from my trick pockets. On my left was Gleniffer's latest toy. Basically, it was a hand drill with a diamond bit. The idea was that it would be driven through a major conduit near the AI centre and take a sample of the nano stream. When, or if, I got it back, the backroom boys and girls should be able to black box the events all the way back to the city going from servant to whatever it was now. In the right holster was the stiletto. It was all I had against everyone.

I sat for a while purposely doing nothing except watching the streets and planning my way to the AI block and then back out. I had memorised the street plan, but you have to watch for a while. You have to know a place from ground level. I paid for another cup of coffee. There was no way around that. My credit chip would probably give me away no matter that it had been built around a New Talinn identity. It was a ploy that worked for a while. Eventually the city would register that there were two identities with the same name, address and credit balance. Every time I interacted with a data silo I made my life just a little more dangerous.

"May I sit here? It's kind of crowded."

My hand tightened on the cup, it was momentary but noticeable. I hadn't expected someone to talk to me. A fair, neat woman about my own age was standing politely at my table. She was fair with shoulder-length hair, softly spoken and well dressed in soft and understated clothing. Suburban family type written all over her. I indicated the chair across from me and let her sit. I had no reason to believe that this was a random act. The AIs learn.

She was well chosen; small and fine featured, with a touch of the good student about her. I tried to will my heartbeat down to a normal level, but it just wouldn't go there.

The influenced are just like you and me. Mostly. The vast majority of the time they are the people they were, they do the same things, go to the same places. The city only controls them when it needs them. It's a solution to the world we inhabit and its unceasing threat. Let's imagine you are a huge leviathan of data and human-to-AI interfaces. Your brain is enormous, multi-faceted and unceasing. It is part of every patient on life support, every patrolman checking the ID's of felons, every call and every message and every choice. It is responsible for holding all that in its control. All that as well as its survival. But that enormous network needs something: it needs limbs. Flicking up those shields is limited, sometimes slow, and sometimes it fails. It needs controllable armatures within. It needs muscles to flex when the time comes to defend itself. The city, after all, was built as a fortress against our new world. It was built to do it intelligently, to find improved solutions. And so, it did.

She looked at me quite directly. It wasn't something women did. Not on such brief acquaintance.

I am not confident with women. I am not good looking nor am I charming. I'm certainly not funny. Sure, I think that some people like me but that's as far as it goes. There was a possibility that she would cross the room for me, but it was very small. The auto served her coffee and she looked down and took it seriously. Powdered cream and sugar were measured and added. She concentrated all the way through the little performance. A piece of ordinariness that would be an unthinking and even ignored act in the uninfluenced.

Sometimes there is nothing to do except be direct. "You want to talk?" I asked.

That question would usually make people uncomfortable, but she gave me an equally plain answer. "Yes, I'd like to talk. I'm Ursula." Her augment was mostly under a curl of fair hair. Just below the skin the nanos from that augment were interfacing with interrelated data far beyond human capacity. It had been a good servant, not too long ago. She smiled. Ursula was a lovely woman, the kind I would have liked to know.

"I'm Peter," I said. There was no longer much point in game-playing. My charade was done. "Who am I talking to?"

"Someone like you."

True but meaningless. "Am I talking to the city?"

"No, I'm Ursula. Just like I told you. The city can't talk. It can't understand."

"What does it do?"

"It just protects, and it maintains."

That made me smile. That was the motto of Central Admin, the faceless black block that was the centre of the city. *To Protect and to Maintain.* I admired its simplicity.

"How did you find me?"

"A breach event was correlated with a variety of other events. Simple things. Even that here, you are a new customer." Ursula shrugged. "The leap, the guesswork was the human part."

"In a city this size there must be thousands of correlations. Newness events." I looked around the little café. "Even new customers."

"There are."

"Which must have generated a lot of Ursulas. May I ask you a question?"

"Of course." She tilted her head to the side; I don't think it meant anything, it was just a habit that she already had. That Ursula had.

"What is it like?"

She didn't hesitate. "It's better. It's direct and clear. Life is successful here, Peter. More than it was before."

"That's how it looks."

Her hands were shifting, touching, controlling, moving the coffee cup to... what? Was she trying to place it at an angle? Make it perfect? Or was it just a fruitless activity, the kind of thing anxious people do. That's what I've been told, kindly, always kindly, "Peter, you're wasting time on fruitless activity." That's the kind of thing someone has said to me since I was a child. Now, I knew what it looked like.

"Look around," she said. "Just ordinary people doing ordinary things. No one's life is really changed. Take a walk. Look all you want. There's nothing to be afraid of."

She touched my hand. It felt good. "It's direct and sincere."

I thought of the human torn apart just because she came from beyond the barrier. "Sincere? Odd choice of words."

"It's absolute."

Gleniffer always told me not to over-analyse. But there was something. The city was trying to talk to me, convince me. Why? I was just a bug. Was the city afraid? Afraid of the overwrite I could order? Could it know that we've killed two cities before. AIs share information. Gleniffer calls it contamination and infection but it isn't, not to the cities; it's sharing. It's the expansion of order.

"It's beautiful here, Peter."

It was.

Outside, in a staging area near the barrier, Gleniffer's company would be setting up snub-nosed injection weapons and checking the actions on their carbines. Every man and woman tense as wire, waiting for the order. The first wave will pierce the city's armoured outer layer then inject molten metal to set the wound open. Next, they'll pump nanophage straight into the city systems. That will be the beginning of the city's death. The nanophage go through the urban control matrix slowly but surely, destroying the integrated links – both application and nano particle, then, as the city shudders, those same nanophage, or at least the results of their replication, will find a way – and they always find a way - to get into the human system, the subcutaneous array. The link between the citizen and the city. Then the human dying will start.

The first time we tried it was in Castile. We thought that it would just kill the central AI and its associated nano culture. The idea was that the Castilians would shake their heads and recover. We would walk through the city portal and be treated like liberators. When the assault was over there was hardly anyone left to welcome us at all. The Castilians were reduced to huddles of shapeless dead with blood trickling from their mouths and noses.

We still haven't found a better way. And we don't have the time or the talent to find one.

No one ever says it, but I don't think Gleniffer wants those people back. I think that's why he was chosen. He will allow no variations on humanity.

"Ursula… " I wanted to talk, and it was easy to talk to her. I was also scared. My instincts told me to run, get back to the breach. I looked over her shoulder, just to take my eyes from her flat gaze. I needed to think of a way out. Outside it was wet. It rains a lot in New Talinn, it's a city of light rain through sun and thin clouds. It's always silver skyed and wet underfoot. People walked, some together, some alone, talking through their augments rather than to each other. I kept my eyes on the streets. Ursula was still talking. I heard the gentle buzz of her voice. A calm and steady voice. I never finished the sentence. On the far sidewalk, a couple of the city patrol were bending over, looking at something. One was a woman, fit and athletic, the other, an older man, gaining middle-aged weight and slower in lowering himself to the sidewalk. Typical patrol. At their feet there was a red stain, dark like wine on the ground. It was spreading and thinning in the wet. The cops were looking at flesh. A torn mass of blood and flesh that had been a human being. It must have happened before I stepped into the coffee shop. Maybe it happened while I was there, and I was so self-absorbed I didn't notice. Often, we don't notice an event – just the reaction to it. But there was no reaction.

No one stopped, no one screamed in horror. I would have stared. Anyone would have stared. That pile of flesh was once human. It was torn to those remains by other humans. Nothing else could have done that. We have no wild animals except ourselves. And it was nothing, nothing to anyone. Everyone in New Talinn was walking past. That person, that lost person, was Other, Outrider, Divergence.

Why was no one hysterical? Why was no one looking for someone lost?

Ursula drew her hands back from the cup. It was half-empty. By the looks of it, exactly half-empty. "Peter? What are you going to do?"

I needed a useful lie. I couldn't think of anything.

In the right holster I had the stiletto. It was a thin blade twelve centimetres long and filled with nanophage. I'd never used it. Didn't even know if it worked. I couldn't give Ursula the right answer. The wrong answer was going to leave me just like that pile of flesh outside in the rain.

I was isolated and scared. I had been before, but this was a different quality of fear. I was going to kill Ursula. She was still human. I'd never killed anyone before. But I didn't want to die, and I didn't want to die that way, having the people turn on me like white blood cells on antigen.

"Peter, what are you going to do? You overwrote Castile. Ninety-eight thousand, two hundred and twenty-two people."

Even her number was exact. It didn't matter. There was no Ursula, not in the full sense. I wondered if, in another life, Ursula would have sat next to me. The real Ursula.

Using the stiletto would buy time. Just time.

The nanophage are fast, the effect isn't instantaneous, but it is quick. Her augment would send out an error message eventually but by that time I would be gone. The payload of the stiletto was a one-time deal. After that, all I had was the steel.

"Ursula..." I drew it and kept my arm under the table. I put my free hand on top of her arm. I made the movement soft and affectionate. She turned her head slightly. I pushed the point forward with one fast action. It was easier than I thought it would be. I held her tight.

I softened my voice. I'm always too loud, especially when I'm scared. "I'm sorry."

Ursula changed before she died. I can't explain it, but I saw it. Her face changed from the city to Ursula. An Ursula I had never met before, never spoken to before and who was not the city. It was beautiful, there was warmth there, like a woman who was happy and complete.

It's important not to run. The city does not understand crime or murder except as a statistic or a hygiene issue. But it learns. It correlates. It finds your raised heartbeat, your panicked progress down the wrong street, it feels you pressing the crossing button again and again even when it doesn't make any difference. It picks up your pheromones and models your too-fast walk from every environmental sensor, every enhanced camera. It builds a picture of you, isolates you from every other spike in the data and eventually, given long enough, its extremities will find you.

Don't take cars, don't take public transport. Keep away from anything that might want to imprint you, measure you or observe you.

I wanted off the streets and into green spaces. Parks wound through every uptown neighbourhood. Keeping to those meadows and woodlands that snaked through residential streets had worked before. I walked, and I walked slowly. The urge to run was so strong that I could hardly fight it. I watched my feet as they stepped down onto the grass in front of me. I counted my own footsteps. It gave me something regular, something manageable to think about.

It was cool and dry in the park. I cleared my mind, calmed down as much as I could. Far behind me I could hear a patrol siren. Funny how the city does ordinary things, like calling cops to a killing. It's a reflection of who we are, of who made it.

I don't know how long it took to get to the city barrier. It must have taken nearly an hour. I avoided people and human noise. The city was hunting me even if I couldn't see it. Eventually I found myself near the monorail stop. At least I was close. I could just see the ugly armour of the city's edge rise over a screen of tall pines.

There were people amongst the trees. They did not look like people making themselves ready for pursuit or violence. I can spot the adrenalised movements of a violent crowd. No, they were just strolling or standing, some chatting into their augment. I stopped and took to one knee. If I was right, then I should have been within shouting distance of Fordyce's breach. But it looked like I would have to get through a ring of the city's influenced. They were just passive, ordinary citizens right now. But there was no doubt they were forming a cordon. The stiletto was all I had.

It was close to the time for Fordyce to blast an exit breach. Even when he did trigger the cutter, that didn't mean I could get to the hole. Maybe he would sense something. Maybe Gleniffer had ordered another flyover. All I could do was wait in the shade of the pines.

It was so fast when it happened. They went from nothing to everything. Just a rush of noise and hands straight at me. It's overwhelming, the impact, the weight of bodies, the feeling of being prey. Hands everywhere, pulling, clawing. They made no noise. Shouting and screaming, venting through voice wasn't needed. Human excess such as vocalization in violence was not required. I hit out as hard as I could. I knocked one down. They kept grabbing and I kept hitting the way Fordyce taught me, simple repeat shots to the head.

I hit with elbows, knees, anything to get space. You don't last long against that mass and chaotic violence. I was down to my last few seconds and I knew it.

I drew the stiletto and found a target. Straight into the heart and pumped the blade. He dropped, and I twisted round for another. The smell of blood was added to the smell of humans, of their skin and sweat. I was pushed down to my knees. I could feel the skin of my face being pulled.

From somewhere behind me I heard a blast, sharp, fast and low. I could hear noise, clipped military sounds of shouted orders. One was Fordyce's bull voice among the dull sounds of impact and falling. My ears roared, and I wasn't fully aware of anything. Someone pulled me out from the mass of bodies. I saw Fordyce's face. He was shouting something, but I couldn't answer. I was half-crazy. They dragged me back to the breach away from the clawing hands. There were bodies near the trees.

Fordyce was shouting that we had to get out through. Then he was talking to me. He had to repeat himself before I understood. "Do we kill it?"

"Kill it."

Gleniffer helped walk me back.

I sat on the grass in the prairie breeze and let the blood harden on my skin. The assault was already in its early stages. Files of green-uniformed assault troops hauled equipment forward. They moved with the interlocking surety of practice. First the breaching squads, then the nanophage into the city's conduits. After that, infantry would pour through. It would be methodical and clinical.

Gleniffer leaned against his carrier, watching his green ants overrun the citadel. "You did good, Peter. It's a full overwrite."

Eighty thousand souls. Seventy-eight thousand, four hundred and seventy to be exact.

Gleniffer looked pleased; a man of action in the thick of it. They picked the right man. The infestation and Gleniffer suited each other. Both contagion of the other and the cure finally able to face each other on the field of battle. His face was lit up, a man with a mission and a divine purpose.

The overwrite would be absolute.

During the day, **Raymond W Gallacher** is a technical writer for an IT company in Linlithgow, Scotland. He is married with two children and thinks up ideas while walking the family dog. Raymond has always loved good speculative fiction and, after a significant life turnaround, took the plunge and enrolled at Glasgow University to study the novel and the short story.

2019 Shoreline of Infinity Flash Fiction Competition— the prize winners!

Winner
Simon Fung – Those Who live by the Shawarma

Runners-up
Emma Levin – Search History
Anna Ziegelhof – Dimenso-yarn Ad Copy, draft

Simon's story is a worthy winner – here's what the judges say:

"A great twist on reality – and science fiction. I enjoyed the structure. The ability to reduce the twist into one paragraph at the very end, and to do so with such impact on the rest shone through remarkably. However, for me, it was the creativity in producing a twist, utterly bizarre yet completely relatable and comprehensible, which won this prize."

"A great story I have read over and over again and has been lingering in my mind even now. Well done."

"There is something truly admirable for when a story can sneak up on you as much as an event can sneak up on a character – I was drawn into a false sense of security reading this story and will be haunted by it for months to come!"

On Anna's tale:

"The interesting and unique structure feels as though there are multiple stories going on at once. But better yet, well executed because it remains comprehensible and engaging."

"Creative in content, style, and tone, this story is unlike any piece I'd read before. This piece is truly unique and addictive to read, but even after the tenth time, it doesn't lose its charm or humour!"

Emma's short piece:

"Great structure. A definite twist on the short story, told through the protagonist's search history. The cyclicity also left an interesting twist at the end for me to think about."

"This story is a hilarious piece, drawing on our innate curiosity and stubbornness during the DIY process!"

Simon Fung wins a cash prize of £50 and a a one-year subscription to the digital edition of Shoreline of Infinity magazine. Emma Levin and Anna Zeigelhof receive a one-year subscription to the digital edition of Shoreline of Infinity.

Thanks go to our judges:

Dodo Charles, Emma Hughes, Elizabeth Park, Tamara Price, Eryn Rigley, Rachel Wood

the brilliant students taking English Literature at Edinburgh University. They took to the task with diligence and commitment, and were a joy to work with.

Thanks go to Dr Simon Malpas, Senior Lecturer of Edinburgh University who organised and supported the team of judges. Also thanks to Pippa Goldschmidt for her 'how to be a story competition judge' chat at the first meeting of the judges.

If you want to listen to these stories, use the QR code or visit: www.shorelineofinfinity.com/soi17-e

—*Noel Chidwick*
Editor
Shoreline of Infinity

Search History

Emma Levin

VR Headset
Cheap VR Headset
Cheap and Good VR Headset
Argos voucher code
Argos North Bridge Opening Times

VR Headset not working
VR Headset error code 27b/6
VR error "unit already in use"
Argos Customer Services Number
Samsung Customer Care Number (product in warranty)
How to complain about customer services

VR what does "unit already in use" mean
Error 27b/6 but I'm not using another VR headset
Reddit VRChat
Foster Conspiracy
Foster Conspiracy wiki
Foster VR implants in children

How to relax

Best parks in Edinburgh
Weather today
Citymapper
Pizza near me
Voucher Pizza Hut
Have they changed recipe at Pizza Hut?

Define Paranoia
paranoia NHS
Are conspiracy theorists ever right?
Foster VR implant children
How small can they make VR implants
How to tell if someone is lying to you
How to remove VR Implants
VR implant removal always fatal?
How to switch off VR implants
What is 'faraday cage'?
Metalworkers in Edinburgh
Cheap Metalworkers in Edinburgh
Cheap and Good Metalworkers in Edinburgh
Is £400 normal for a callout fee
How to build a Faraday cage
Chicken Wire Amazon
Wire cutters Amazon
Beekeeping mask Amazon
Pizza hut voucher

How to cut chicken wire
What do if cut self with chicken wire
Hw tostopp bleedng
Wont stpp bleedng
WHat is tourniquet
How to get blood out of carpet

Amazon gloves for cutting chicken wire

What happens when you get in Faraday cage
Why don't people smile
Why is there so much rubbish on the streets
Why is the sky grey
Is the sky always this grey
Why is the world awful?
Why is no one doing anything about it?

Can you make yourself forget something
Hypnotherapy wiki
Does hypnotherapy work
Hypnotherapists Edinburgh
Cheap Hypnotherapists Edinburgh
Cheap and Good Hypnotherapists Edinburgh
How to clear search history

.

..

...

VR Headset
Cheap VR Headset
Cheap and Good VR Headset
Argos voucher code
Argos North Bridge Opening Times

Emma Levin's short stories have appeared in anthologies (e.g. *England's Future History*), magazines (e.g. *Thousand Zine*), and many, many recycling bins. She currently lives in London, and was on the BBC's 'Comedy Room' writers' development scheme for 2018-19

Dimenso-yarn ad copy, draft

Anna Ziegelhof

+@Nadine: great first task for you! This ad copy came back from the freelancer; see if it can be salvaged. Thx, Serena.

When the other universe first appeared, access to the universe beyond the rift was for scientists only. Us normal people, we couldn't go. But the scientists needed coffee and food, so Starbucks made its move. Starbucks is the great equalizer of course.

+@Serena: suggest striking above paragraph; nothing new here, not related to product, overly focused on Starbucks brand (or do we have a collaboration with Starbucks?)

Next, the novelty of doing research in another universe began to wear off and the scientists got bored, despite living right across from the stunning aurora borealis in the rift. Casinos, movie theaters, strip clubs and their employees were allowed across the rift to entertain the scientists.

+@Serena: suggest striking mention of strip clubs

Funding for science is always caught in an uneasy relationship between the greater good, the abstract idea beyond monetization, and the product that can be sold to another being in late capitalism, who is just bored out of their fucking mind and has no other way to ease their ennui than to self-improve by shopping. Mattress stores and fountain-pen subscriptions entered the as yet bare market of the other universe.

Because science found that the other universe was pretty much just a slightly emptier copy of this universe, there weren't that many monetizable research findings: who wants what they already have? Research was declared pointless and ceased.

The universe across the rift opened to tourists. It started to look a bit like Las Vegas over there. These days, there's Little-Las-Vegas inside a hotel in the other universe, and there is Little-Paris-Las-Vegas inside Little-Las-Vegas and we at Dimenso-yarn understand that our entanglement with an inexplicable other universe full of meaningless copies can be overwhelming. So we have created a product, obsessively engineered to help you disentangle your life and create something truly real.

+@Serena: 'ennui', 'monetization', 'late capitalism' are big words, don't read easily, suggest striking for readability

+@Nadine: you don't see anything else wrong with the three (!) paragraphs above?

+@Serena: 'truly real' is redundant; passage is a bit ranty, long sentences; includes 'fucking', may need to test re: target group / Dimenso-yarn branding

+@Nadine: we do not use the words 'late capitalism' while trying to generate revenue. Let's discuss in person at earliest convenience

We know that to live your best life in any dimension, you've got to transcend your ennui, so place yourself back in control of your universe and create something meaningful that will weave a beautiful thread to connect you and your loved ones.

+@Serena: again, strike 'ennui', replace with 'self'; good emotional appeal to 'loved ones'

Father's Day is coming up, so sign up today and receive your first yarn bundle complete with instructions at fifty percent off. Go on, knit Dad that sweater he has always wanted yet never just bought for himself.

We are Dimenso-yarn: the first inter-dimensional online personalized yarn subscription service for the rift-traveler who has it all twice. Put a twist into the known universe.

+@Serena: love the catchphrase, 'Put a twist...' genius, definitely keep that. Move this paragraph to beginning?

+@Nadine: please flag this freelancer as 'will not hire' in our database

With thousands of patterns and colors you can create something unique with your own hands. The universes may be folding into one another and we may be losing our grip on what's real, but *you* can tangle a twist of yarn into an intricate knot that's definitely your own. Ease your existential anxiety! Master the chaos! Dimenso-yarn!

+@ Serena: 'Master the chaos!' another great catchphrase; advise keeping

+@ Nadine: come see me in my office right now

Anna Ziegelhof grew up in Germany and has lived in a succession of other countries. She holds degrees in English, Jewish Studies, and Sociology and has worked as a teacher, translator, and editor. She currently resides in Northern California where she works in tech, devours fiction, and occasionally writes, too.

Those who live by the shawarma

Simon Fung

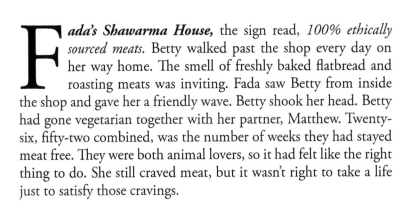

Fada's Shawarma House, the sign read, *100% ethically sourced meats*. Betty walked past the shop every day on her way home. The smell of freshly baked flatbread and roasting meats was inviting. Fada saw Betty from inside the shop and gave her a friendly wave. Betty shook her head. Betty had gone vegetarian together with her partner, Matthew. Twenty-six, fifty-two combined, was the number of weeks they had stayed meat free. They were both animal lovers, so it had felt like the right thing to do. She still craved meat, but it wasn't right to take a life just to satisfy those cravings.

Art: Emily Simeoni

Arriving home, Betty started dinner. She was making Matt's favourite: red lentil curry with a side of salad. He was going to come home for dinner tonight before heading back to the office. Matt had been so busy lately; important business meetings with international clients. Betty was so proud of him. Betty inhaled the aroma of garlic, onions and peppers as she sautéed them; the smells of cooking were invigorating. They had both been feeling so much healthier since they began eating fresh food. Betty hummed happily as she cooked.

The phone rang just as the curry finished simmering. It was Matt.

"Babe, I won't be able to make it home for dinner again, something's come up at work."

Betty was disappointed but tried not to let it show in her voice.

"Do you want me to drop some dinner off for you?"

"No, you stay home," said Matt, "I couldn't ask you to come all the way here just to drop off food."

"It's really not a problem," Betty insisted.

"I'll be fine. I won't be back until tomorrow morning."

He hung up. Betty returned to the kitchen. Some of the lentils had started to stick to the bottom of the pot but she didn't care. She doled out a portion onto rice and sat down in the kitchen to her meal. It should have been spicy, aromatic and warming, but she wasn't in the mood to taste any of it.

Betty grazed mechanically on the salad until she spotted the memory stick sitting next to the fruit bowl. She stopped. Swallowed. That was Matt's memory stick. He needed that for his presentation tonight. Betty took the memory stick, packed the curry and rice into a reheatable box and set off for Matt's workplace with a smile on her lips.

Betty gave Dave, the security guard, a wave. He pressed the button to let her in.

"Bringing Matthew dinner again?" Dave asked.

Betty nodded.

"And his presentation," she added.

Dave grinned. "What would he do without you?"

Betty grinned. She went through the gates towards the lift and selected the eighth floor. The building was quiet after hours. As the lift climbed, Betty imagined how happy Matt would be to see her after a hard day's work. She adjusted her curly white locks so that her hair was just right. The lift opened to an empty office space. The room was dark, save for the light that peeked out from under the door of the far office. She heard muffled sounds coming from that direction. As Betty took a step out of the lift, an ominous feeling gripped her. She stepped closer and heard a woman giggle. She stopped, heart racing. Then she heard Matt's voice. Another step. She heard a soft moan. Betty hurriedly crossed the rest of the distance to the door and barged in. Her senses took in everything. Paperwork pushed off a desk onto the floor. The surprised gasps. The smell of cheap perfume.

Matt frantically tried to put his trousers back on, while the woman hurriedly pulled her shirt over her exposed udders.

"Betty, w-what are you doing here?" said Matt.

"I brought you your favourite: red lentil curry!"

Betty flung the curry at Matt's face. She threw his memory stick on the floor and crunched it under her heel, then stormed out.

The anger didn't last. Tears stung Betty's eyes as she walked home. She felt broken and betrayed. As she walked, she was hit by the familiar smell of roasting meats. Twenty-six weeks. That was how long she had gone without meat for that bastard. She walked into *Fada's Shawarma House*. Fada smiled as she came in; his smile turned to a sympathetic frown.

"Betty, what has happened? You must tell me."

"Matt... he's ... he's been cheating on me."

Betty let out a sob, then burst into tears.

"That swine!" said Fada.

He came around the counter, put an arm around her and helped her to a seat. She couldn't get any more words out and continued sobbing. Fada disappeared for a moment and then came back holding juicy slices of lamb wrapped in fresh flatbread.

"Eat," he urged, "you will feel better, Fada promises."

Betty took the shawarma. Her stomach growled. A small part of her said eating meat was wrong, Matt or no Matt. But the smell was intoxicating. She closed her eyes and bit into the shawarma. The world spun. She felt like she was falling in slow motion, and then reality slammed back into place. Her body felt strange.

"This one here just gave consent," an unfamiliar voice yelled.

Betty slowly opened her eyes. Disorientated. Wires and tubes detached themselves from her head. A feeding tube full of grass juice was pulled from her mouth. Around her, sheep were hooked up to a machine. She looked down in alarm, her hands were hooves. No, her hands had *returned* to being hooves. With the wires gone, the human thoughts began to dissolve.

"Good," another voice said, "take her for processing."

Betty bleated in protest.

The men tried to herd her towards a long line of trucks transporting sheep. But she didn't want to go. Wasn't sure why anymore. There was writing on the side of the truck. It read: *Fada's Shawarma House, 100% ethically sourced meats.*

Simon is a scientist at the University of Leicester; he spends his days finding reasons to turn things fluorescent. Some of his science writing is most certainly fictional, especially if it's the University's Biological Safety Officer asking. You can find him liking cat pictures on Twitter @SimonFung7.

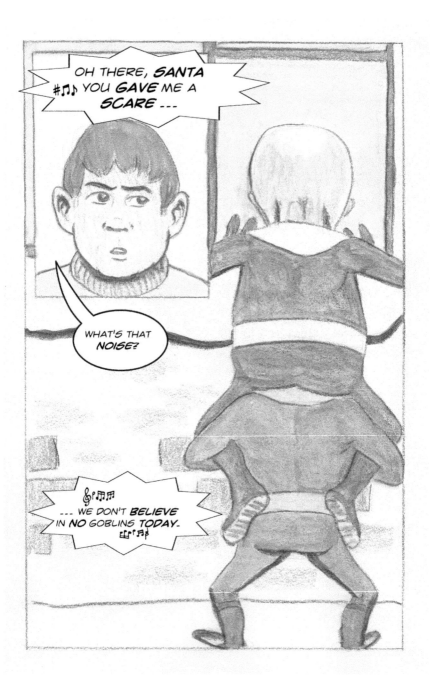

The artists behind the brushes

Siobhan McDonald is a graduate of Dundee University, and has worked in illustration and animation since 2016. She likes to draw in hidden corners of cafés when she's not working in a studio on a storyboard or comic.
Can be found online at Facebook @symcdCAS Instagram @Symcadoodle

Jackie Duckworth is an illustrator and printmaker based near Cambridge. She studied Illustration at Cambridge School of Art and has worked in a variety of fields including book covers and educational projects. She has exhibited across the UK and abroad.
www.jackieduckworthart.co.uk
Instagram @jackie.duckworth.art

Andrew Owens is from Oxfordshire in the UK, and currently works as a graphic designer and freelance illustrator. He draws and writes a wide range of subjects, from dark fantasy and sci fi graphic novels, to colourful childrens' picture books. Examples of his work can be seen on his Instagram: @theonlyandrewowens
https://www.instagram.com/theonlyandrewowens/

Emily Simeoni is an illustrator and printmaker from Edinburgh. She graduated from Coventry University in 2018 with a degree in Illustration. Currently she is working as a studio assistant at Edinburgh Printmakers. She enjoys exploring fantastical themes and dreamscapes, while combining elements from the past with an imagined future. @simeonimacaroni

It has been rumoured that **Mark Toner** is the avatar of a spaceship orbiting out beyond the Kuiper Belt which is funnelling in creative energies from the wider galactic community but he insists that all of the work in this magazine is drawn by humans.
Mark is at www.spacepilot.scot and @tonertweets.

Mairi Archbold lives in Edinburgh, and for the past year has been selling her art at comic conventions all over Scotland. One of these days she plans to start illustrating her own original stories, but until then she spends her time drawing characters from sci-fi, fantasy and superhero media.
Instagram: @spacecapart

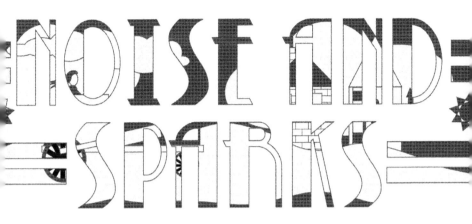

NOISE AND SPARKS

The Elephant in the Ceremony Room

Ruth EJ Booth

It was a moment that lit the blue touch paper under the Science Fiction community: at the 2019 Hugo Awards ceremony in Dublin, Hong Kong British author Jeannette Ng accepted the then John W. Campbell Award for Best New Writer with the words, "So John W. Campbell was a fascist…" The room exploded. The community soon followed.

The award body, to their credit, responded immediately, renaming it the *Astounding* Award after the magazine at which Campbell made his name as an editor. Ng would be the last author to ever bear the stain of his name on their prize. Since then, the genre has moved with speed. The Gunn Center for the

Study of Science Fiction at the University of Kansas has already renamed its annual conference, with its own Campbell award, given to novels, to follow suit.[1] The James Tiptree, Jr. Award, meanwhile, is changing to the Otherwise Award – though some commenters such as S. Qiouyi Lu have pointed out this has its own problems even before we get to the use of the term 'othering' in academic discourse.

Predictably, these moves were not met without criticism. Some called Ng ungrateful and declared the *Astounding* change as tantamount to erasing history. Others wondered why it had taken so long to happen – after all, Ng was not the first to publicly note Campbell's fascist outlook.[2] Yet, these are interesting times for the genre: "science fiction is having a reckoning with its past and its present," as Cory Doctorow recently put it.[3] As John Scalzi also notes, the Campbell award's name change was the result of "long-standing whisper network[s]" becoming "shout[s]" in the wake of Ng's speech.[4] So, even for the majority of people outside of those networks – who are perhaps less aware of the Golden Age than of this, our current second Golden Age, our Platinum Age, of Science Fiction – once those shouts were loud enough to hear, this change became inevitable.

And yet, this moment and its attendant controversy begs another broader question about awards and figureheads in the history of genre. We count on Science Fiction, Fantasy and Horror awards not only to reflect the best of their genres, but the best of us – our values, and what our community stands for. But in a world very much in flux, how can we be sure that an award, or its awarding, really means what we intend? As we move out of award season 2019 and into 2020, perhaps it's time we addressed the elephant in the ceremony room: not just how do we choose the names of genre awards, but in doing so what do we want our awards to stand for?

Of course, this is more of an issue for some awards than others. Awards given by bodies such as the British Fantasy Society or British Science Fiction Association are simply named for the organisation awarding them, granting both the stability of an historical establishment and the ongoing development that an ever-fluctuating membership provides. If you don't agree with an award, then it's simply what the collective (or their representative jury) decided on this year (although this does leave the stickier problem of what exactly we mean when we say a work is the 'best'). Meanwhile, award organizations without an established society behind them are left to choose their own name – one that embodies the heart of what they stand for, while setting them apart from their contemporaries. One that establishes them as exciting, unique: an award that any author would be thrilled to receive, any publisher delighted to shout about; yet simultaneously authentic to genre and rooted in its history or aspirations.

From that perspective, authors would seem to make wonderful namesakes for literature awards. When their works make great strides in our collective understanding, authors often become touchstones for explorations of particular topics. Why not ride on the coattails of a famous writer in naming your award, and

Ruth makes Noise and Sparks as BFS award winner

We're delighted to share the great news that Ruth EJ Booth won this year's prize for best non-fiction at the British Fantasy Society's awards for her Noise and Sparks column in Shoreline of Infinity. She was presented with her trophy at the recent British Fantasy Society Awards ceremony at FantasyCon.

pic: E M Faulds

Ruth joined us for Shoreline of Infinity 4, the 2016 issue, where in her first column, 'Carrying Glass', she reflected on what it means to a writer to receive an award, and be acknowledged. In Shoreline of Infinity 11, our all-women issue dedicated to International Women's Day, Ruth provided an insightful look at creating real women characters in fiction. 'Beyond the Mountains' is a thoughtful lesson for all writers, packed into 1,000 words.

My joy as editor is to watch for her columns popping up in my email box – so I get to read them first!

Ruth well deserves this award – and the further recognition that comes with it.

capitalise on their familiarity and authenticity? Indeed, as with the formerly titled Tiptree, which is dedicated to works pushing the frontiers of our understanding of gender, often the memory of these authors prompts the setting up of these awards in the first place.

The problem comes when the names we choose don't just stand for the values we assign them. The naming of an award after a person often comes long after they have passed away, when cultural memory has crystalised around them and what they represent to a specific genre. Historiography often betrays us: we like to put authors on pedestals and name them figureheads, as quick and easy ciphers for key points in the past. But those who shape history don't always make great strides because they embody the best of us. Consider the other awards given out the night of Ng's Campbell award, the ones named after Hugo Gernsback – the creator of the first magazine dedicated to Science Fiction, *Amazing Stories*, but also a man known for paying his writers extremely badly, if at all, and with his own racist past.[5]

If that's true, then suppose we simply take a leaf out of the book of those who argue for the status quo: focus on the achievements of namesakes and agree to forget their unsavoury sides. Treat them like an old racist great-uncle – what the science fiction genre has been doing for decades, in the case of Campbell. So, how do you guarantee that everyone else sees only the positive side of their contributions to genre? That they don't also see the trauma this author caused? That they aren't a victim of it themselves? How can you be certain they don't believe that with receiving this award comes a tacit agreement: to sweep their trauma under the rug, grit their teeth, and smile politely through the pain?

There's been a lot of discussion in recent years about how we handle revelations about those we consider role models, and the relationship between art and artist. Even if we divorce the two, an artist's contributions to genre may still be affected by their prejudices. To suggest that, by casting the artist into the past, the trauma they cause is somehow reduced by being historical is to deny the fresh harm that occurs every time their attitudes are encountered again. Indeed, attempting to divorce art from the artist in this way speaks to the privilege behind declarations such as "yes, I understand the man is a dreadful racist, but he's always been kind to me."

None of this destroys the historical contributions of authors to speculative genres. Awards are not the only way to remember contributions to history. Universities and colleges still teach of the works of problematic authors with warnings about their perspectives. To continue to read them is a matter of personal choice. However,

"There's been a lot of discussion in recent years about how we handle revelations about those we consider role models"

when we step onto the world stage, those matters cease to be personal. When we choose a person's name for an award, we take all that they were into that prize, including what they mean to those within and outside of our genre. Whether standing for a progressive future, or carrying forward the legacies of the past, we must ask ourselves whether an award can ever afford to be a 'problematic fave.'

Our path seems clear, then – we only name awards after people whose pasts we have scrutinized, who we are sure will represent the ideals of that award. Yet humans are particularly tricky in that respect. How can we guarantee there are no skeletons in their closets that could tarnish the award and what it represents?

The fact is, we can't. Human beings make mistakes. We try and fail. Most people are not fascists, but rare is the person whose life perfectly embodies an ideal or a campaign, especially within the institutionalised biases of western society. Much as with Naomi Klein's recent comments on climate change movements, it is very difficult for those advocating for a better world not to be hypocrites by living in this one.[6]

And this is the fundamental issue with naming an award after a person. Artists, by their very nature, are constantly growing, often changing views and perspectives across their lives: indeed, it's often their greatest strength. Awards, on the other hand, are intended to consistently embody the highest ideals of humanity or artistry. By naming awards after authors, we expect them to be unchanging ciphers for these ideals – in short, something other than what they are.

Almost always, there will be some aspect of an author's past that makes them unsuitable as the namesake for an award. So perhaps we should take a cue from the art they create instead. Authors of Science Fiction and Fantasy create new worlds not just to reflect on our society, but to show us new paths to take, new ways to be. Likewise, awards should be named as new creations in themselves, names that represent a fresh way forward and who we hope to become as a community: in this way, not just honouring our legendary authors, but the better worlds for which they often stood.

Endnotes

1 The announcement was made via the Gunn Center's Facebook page on 5th September 2019 here: https://www.facebook.com/GunnCenter/posts/3037499232933336 [accessed 3 November 2019].

2 John Scalzi reports Michael Moorcock said it in accepting the award as early as 1971: https://whatever.scalzi.com/2019/09/06/the-gunn-center-makes-a-change-and-further-thoughts-on-the-reassessment-of-john-w-campbell/ [accessed 3 November 2019].

3 See Cory Doctorow's column for Locus, 'Jeannette Ng Was Right: John W. Campbell Was a Fascist': https://locusmag.com/2019/11/cory-doctorow-jeannette-ng-was-right-john-w-campbell-was-a-fascist/ [accessed 5 November 2019].

4 For John Scalzi's blog on this, see https://whatever.scalzi.com/2019/09/06/the-gunn-center-makes-a-change-and-further-thoughts-on-the-reassessment-of-john-w-campbell/ [accessed 3 November 2019].

5 See Ryan P. Smith's retrospective on Gernsback's career here: https://www.smithsonianmag.com/smithsonian-institution/fifty-years-later-remembering-sci-fi-pioneer-hugo-gernsback-180964554/ [accessed 6 November 2019].

6 For a clip from Naomi Klein's recent interview with Krishnan Guru-Murthy, see https://twitter.com/channel4news/status/1184505390404374530 [accessed 3 November 2019].

Ruth EJ Booth is a BFS and BSFA award-winning writer and academic based in Glasgow, Scotland. She can be found online at www.ruthbooth.com, or on twitter at @ruthejbooth.

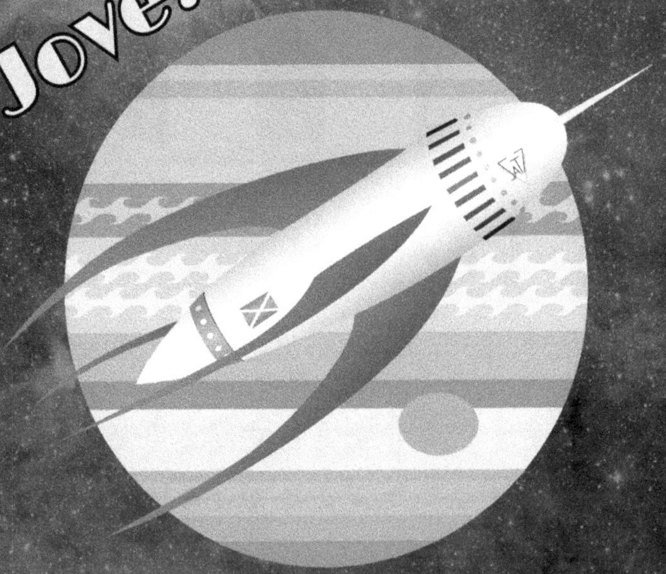

Chris Beckett

Joanna McLaughlin: What are the key themes you were keen to explore in Beneath the World, a Sea?

Chris Beckett: I really wanted to write a book in which my unconscious mind got as much opportunity as possible to do its thing through the actions and thoughts of the characters, so I deliberately started out with rather less of a preconception of what the book was going to be about

than I normally do. But I suppose the unconscious was a key theme, the way that our minds are compartmentalised, and the way that there is always a 'shadow' side of us, a hidden side that's almost the opposite of the way we present ourselves and the way that we like to imagine ourselves to be.

JM: The idea of there being a 'hidden side' to people feels particularly relevant in today's world given how much of

Shoreline's **Joanna McLaughlin** talks to Chris Beckett

Chris Beckett is a university lecturer living in Cambridge.
He has written over 20 short stories, many of them originally
published in Interzone and Asimov's. He is the winner of the Edge
Hill Short Story competition, 2009, for The Turing Test, as well
as the prestigious Arthur C. Clarke award, 2013, for Dark Eden.
Beneath the World, A Sea is out now in hardback and will be
available in paperback in March 2020.

Shoreline of Infinity would like to thank the publishers, Atlantic
Books (http://corvus-books.co.uk), for their help with this
interview, and providing the extract.

our communications/ human
engagement currently takes
place online. These platforms
seem to simultaneously create
a pressure to portray yourself as
living the 'perfect life', while at
the same time providing a sense
of anonymity that allows people
the freedom to say things that
they never would in 'real life',
without directly having to deal
with consequences of those
actions. Was this something
that was in your mind when
you were writing this novel?

CB: It wasn't in my mind,
as far as I know, but it's a very
interesting connection to make.
As a result of his river journey,
the main character Ben finds
himself passing through a place
called the Zona, which no one
remembers after they've left it,
and entering the Submundo,
where in various ways, the
forest plucks at the barriers
in people's minds and brings
buried things to the surface.

And at the same time, he's aware that at some point he's going to have to leave all this and return to the 'real' world outside. So yes, it is a bit like the online world in that there are a multiplicity of places which each offer different possibilities in terms of the parts of yourself you can reveal and the parts you need to conceal. In the Zona you can do things which will be hidden even from your own future self.

JM: The novel poses some challenging questions about someone's public persona compared to who they actually are, or fear they could be. Is this sense of 'selves' rather than a 'self' something you were keen to explore in the novel, and by the end, do you think Ben reached some level of acceptance about himself?

CB: I think all of us are much more divided and contradictory than we might appear from the way we present ourselves. (A relatively superficial instance of this would be the fact that people often express somewhat different views, apparently quite sincerely, depending on who they're talking to.) But Ben is particularly divided to the point that he really doesn't know who he is at all and has hitherto tried to get round this by dutifully being what he thinks he ought to be. His dilemma lies in the fact that he fears that the buried part of himself might actually be evil. Should he run the risk of trying to be authentically himself, or should he carry on trying to be good, even though this means to himself and to others, he comes over as bottled-up and inauthentic? I guess he does reach a decision about this towards the end, but we don't know whether it was the right one (assuming that you can even use the words 'right' and 'wrong' in such a context!). All the other main characters – Justine, Hyacinth, Tim, Jael, Rico – have their own approach to this question of how to be authentic, how to be true to oneself, and so does the imaginary culture that I describe in the book, the culture of the Mundinos, who have to find a way of remaining sane individuals in a place which constantly tries to unpick their sense of self.

JM: Do you think that being authentic and remaining true to yourself can be a particular challenge that some writers face? For, example, can writing successful novels in one genre and developing a following of readers ever create unhelpful pressures on writers to continue to publish similar works in the future (even if there may be different subjects they want to explore)?

CB: I think that can be a pressure. I know that people who liked my Eden books won't necessarily want to follow me into the kinds of books I've written since, and I can see why some writers might feel they have to carry on turning out the kinds of books that people seem to want from them. I don't want to do that, but I don't deny that with each new book I wonder if people are going to follow me or not.

The other thing about writing is that it is incredibly exposing. In one way, it's all made-up stuff (in this case imaginary characters in the middle of an imaginary forest that you can only reach by travelling for several weeks up an imaginary river), but however many layers of artifice you put over it, behind it all is you: your attitudes, your assumptions, your experience, your fears and desires and blind spots. You write your story and there it is for anyone to see who chooses to buy the book. You might think that you've hidden yourself very thoroughly, or you might feel that you've boldly laid out who you really are, but in either case, your readers may well not agree. They may easily spot what you thought you'd hidden, or they may see right through what you imagined was authentically you. You really can't control what they will see!

But my own motivation for writing is certainly something to do with a search for authenticity. I never really succeed, but each time I embark on a book, I'm trying to get beneath the surface of myself or beneath the surface of the world.

JM: *While never taking a side, the novel also explores the challenges of trying to impose one country's cultures and values onto a different community or group of people, and the risks of globalisation. Do you think it is becoming increasingly important to consider how we manage this in a responsible way as the world becomes more inter-connected?*

CB: Yes, I'm very interested in all of that. I'm particularly interested in how apparently benign interventions can be destructive, and how benign intentions can serve as a smokescreen to conceal less benign ones, not just from others, but from ourselves. For example, in this story, concern about the needs of one group – the 'duendes' – is used to justify negative attitudes towards another group, the 'Mundinos', by people who don't fully understand their own motives, and certainly don't understand the complexity of the real relationship between duendes and Mundinos. We are in a world where different cultures that formerly existed in relative isolation from one another, are thrown together, and it's very difficult to know how best to manage that, as all the debates about cultural relativism and so forth indicate.

I have no answers, but I'm suspicious of the assumption that the ideas now held by western liberals such as myself, are necessarily superior to belief systems that seem strange and sometimes ugly to me, but which have evolved to deal with situations that I have no experience of.

JM: In Beneath the World, a Sea *you create a very vivid and somewhat unsettling world for Ben to explore, which lets the reader share in his sense of growing unease as its secrets begin to unfold. As a writer, how do you go about creating a new world and is that process different to creating a character?*

CB: That's an interesting question. You know you're getting somewhere with a character when he or she starts making decisions which you hadn't actually planned for. Obviously, a world doesn't normally make decisions, but in a way the same applies. You know you're getting somewhere

with a world when you find yourself adding details which just feel right. This world only came alive for me when I finally decided to set it on Earth and make it reachable by a long river journey rather than, as I originally intended, setting it on another planet. A river journey carries all kinds of associations which a space journey doesn't have, and a river journey into a place where the unconscious rules is almost an archetype, which I suppose has its origins in 19th-century journeys up rivers like the Amazon and the Congo.

JM: How does returning to a world you've already created (such as with the Eden trilogy) compare to creating a whole new world? Is it exciting to return to an existing world and have the opportunity to think through the different ways it could have evolved over time, or do you prefer the chance to start again with the freedom to create something entirely new?

CB: I think there are pros and cons both ways. It was certainly fun to go back to Eden in the second and third books and find new things there, and new places which I hadn't visited before. It makes the world seem very expansive to me, not just a narrow strip of scenes just wide enough to provide a backdrop for a story but almost like a real place,

> **"I'm suspicious of the assumption that the ideas now held by western liberals such as myself, are necessarily superior to belief systems that seem strange to me"**

and that's a truly lovely feeling which I know all SF readers will understand.

And it was fun, too, to have the characters in the second and third books (set a century and a half later than the first) refer back to the events in the first book as a source of stories and meanings in their own lives, because that's how the past works, and it was lovely to be able to make that happen rather than just describe it.

But obviously any given world is restraining after a while, and, though I have a great fondness for Eden (and a special fondness for the third Eden book, *Daughter of Eden*), I don't regret moving on from it. *America City* was set in a near-future North America, so much less world-building was involved, but it was fun in *Beneath the World* to really splash out again on a completely alien environment, and just let my unconscious loose on it until that too felt

to me almost like a real place: the peculiar little town, the winding river, the forest with its magenta trees … If I dip into the book now, it's almost like someone else wrote it about a place that's out there and not just in my head.

JM: What impact has winning the Arthur C. Clarke Award for Dark Eden *had on your career?*

CB: It had a big impact. First of all, the award in itself was a massive boost to my confidence as a writer. But secondly, it (and my previous award for my short story collection, *The Turing Test*) has meant that more people take notice of my work. And after all, whatever some writers might say, we do write because we want to be read!

JM: Do you have any advice for people looking to develop a career in writing? While every writer must dream of winning awards, I imagine a big part of writing life is also preparing yourself for rejection. Do you have any tips on dealing with that side of things?

CB: I think persistence in spite of rejection is a big part of succeeding as a writer. But it is a big gamble. You have to commit yourself to working away at something for a very long period of time, without any guarantee that you'll get anywhere. It's like committing yourself to digging a mine shaft over many years through solid rock, without any guarantee that there's gold down there to be found. In my case, having worked at writing since I was in my teens, I was in my forties before I ever got a book published, and in my middle fifties before I won an award. I'm getting into my stride now, but I'm also getting old! I'll be sixty-four at my next birthday!

And yes, rejection hurts. Writing's very personal, as I said earlier. There's been times when rejection has reduced me to tears because it feels like I've been seen and found wanting. But you just have to try and learn from it.

In any case, if you're like me, there really isn't any choice in the matter. A writer is simply what I am! Or perhaps it's more accurate (if less romantic) to say that being a writer is the only way I've found of solving the problem of not knowing who I am, because it lets me be many different people all at once.

My God, I am getting deep here! Enough! Two practical bits of advice for new writers:

Don't obsess about getting published at the beginning. People do, I've noticed, but that's putting the cart before the horse. The first thing to do is to get good. No one would expect to play piano in a concert hall until they'd really mastered the instrument, and that takes time and work. Sometimes people seem to want to get published when they still haven't got much further than the writing equivalent of playing 'Chopsticks'.

Network. Go to conventions or writers' groups. Get to know small-press publishers, other writers. My big break was getting to know Andrew Hook, who ran a small press at the time (the brilliant Elastic Press) and published my collection, *The Turing Test*. He put it in for a prize and it won, and that was a major step on the way to getting myself published on a larger scale. I only got to know Andrew because I was introduced to him at a convention by another writer, Neil Williamson, who I'd met at a previous convention through other writers again. I met my agent John Jarrold in the same kind of way. Networking won't get you published unless your stuff is good enough, but it will give you people to work with when it is.

Joanna McLaughlin works with local government in Scotland. She is a fan of all things science fiction and springer spaniel.

Beneath the World, a Sea (extract)

Chris Beckett

The sky was glowing in the east with the light of the rising half-moon, and by the time he reached the track into the forest, the moon itself was shining softly through the trees, making those dim spiral shadows on the ground that he'd imagined and longed for as he sat outside the café with Hyacinth. On the far side of a pool, three harts stood watching him with their cold unblinking eyes. A ghost ray flopped its way through the trees. He flipped on his torch to shine in its direction and saw it for a moment head-on, its white body and fleshy wings seeming merely to frame the great, dark, gaping hole where a head should have been.

Keeping his torch switched on, he strode forward, sweeping the beam round hungrily each time he heard a splash from one of the pools or channels. Once a fat blue beetle rattled past him, one of those occasional strays from the world outside, and Ben followed it until it alighted on the trunk of a tree beside the path. At once, tiny, soft white tendrils flowed out from the smooth purple skin of the tree, embracing the creature so gently that it didn't even try to resist, but simply clung on there, twitching its antennae, while the tendrils flowed together to become a membrane. Only when this new white skin tightened did the beetle belatedly realize it was about to suffocate, and the membrane jerked slightly a couple of times as the creature struggled to free itself. But the tree held tight until the insect was still.

He knew Hyacinth was right. There were no predators in the Submundo, no poisonous snakes, no animals that bit or stung, but it was a dangerous place. It might feel benign to someone whose hidden heart longed to reach the surface and open itself up to the world, but it wasn't in any way concerned with human welfare, only with maintaining its ancient hegemony. It cared no more for him than it cared for that beetle, or for that poor bewildered lizard which the bluebirds had pecked to death.

Yes, Ben thought as he plunged on along the track, but that was part of the appeal of it, and that was why Justine's silly little duendes were so repellent. There were other forces in the world than kindness and fairness and you had to embrace them too if you were going to be truly alive.

He found a pool, stripped and dived in. The water was soft and cool against his bare skin as he swam down into the cathedrallike spaces under the forest. But when he surfaced under the root mass, he realized there wasn't going to be a repeat of his time in the wooden cave. He was at a different point. The coolness, the stillness, the merging of himself with the world around him was no longer soothing in the way it had been then because he knew it would soon be beyond his reach, and he would be back home in London, inside the dull little box of his own head, writing reports, attending meetings, punishing himself grimly in the gym. He climbed from the water, left the track and followed a small path south, away from the Lethe and deeper into the forest.

'Come on, you bastards,' he muttered. 'Where are you? You accuse me of hiding but here I am!'

He passed several groups of harts. They watched him silently, impassively, with their faceted eyes, with none of the poised, nervous tension of wild animals in the world outside. One of those flat white ribbon-like creatures flowed across the forest floor in front of him. And then Ben had a sudden sense of something immensely tall and thin walking alongside him, perhaps twenty yards off through the trees, its white face turned towards him. In a moment of pure, irrational terror, he imagined it to be the

Palido of the Mundino legends, the ghost of Baron Valente, with his cold smile, his top hat, his embroidered waistcoat, come to capture and bury him. But his torch beam revealed a completely inhuman creature, with long, thin arms and legs and a spherical and headless body, from which the limbs appeared to dangle as if from a helium balloon that was almost but not quite light enough to float away. Bobbing slightly, just as a balloon would do, the thing stopped, extended its arms sideways, and turned the flats of its many-fingered hands towards him as if they were parabolic dishes. It stayed in that position for several seconds, and then, apparently completing its task, it turned and loped away through the trees with that same strange bobbing gait, as though it was walking on the moon.

The forest creaked softly.

'Where are you?' Ben shouted, sweeping his torch around to create a kind of kaleidoscope of spiral leaves and spiral shadows. But apart from shadows, nothing moved. He wondered if his torch was the problem and turned it off, plunging himself into a world so vague and undefined it barely existed. There were just vague spiral shapes in the dim grey light, and here and there the glow of a pool or a channel. The only thing that was clear and solid was the halfmoon he glimpsed through the leaves, and the sharp black spirals silhouetted against it.

A series of small splashing sounds came from the distance and he peered into the darkness, resisting the temptation to flick his torch on again. But whatever it was that had emerged from the hidden sea, it appeared to have no interest in him, for nothing approached and the silence returned. He waited motionless for several minutes, then continued walking, the spiral shadows passing across his skin as if he was simply a wave of pressure moving through the shadowy fabric of this grey and tenuous world. He came to a pool with a space on one side of it where, for no obvious reason, there were no tree trunks. Suddenly he had the sense once again of a tall, pale presence watching him.

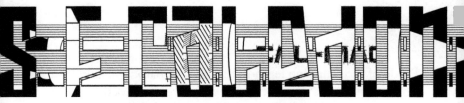

J.T. McIntosh – A Neglected Talent

Tony Quin

In 2016, whilst undertaking voluntary work in the National Library of Scotland, I was introduced to the works of J.T. McIntosh, a Scottish science fiction writer who achieved notable success during the fifties and sixties in both Europe and the USA. He is the only science fiction author whose literary papers are held in the Library, this archive filling some twenty boxes stored on a bank of shelves, several floors below street level. My first reaction was one of embarrassment for I had never heard of J.T. McIntosh. So, I asked around and found, with the exception of the person who purchased the archive in 2010, that no-one else at the Library had heard of him either.

Needless to say, this intrigued me and, having spent two years working on the archive, I have come to the conclusion that J.T. McIntosh was a Scottish science fiction writer of unique talent whose story deserves to be told.

McIntosh was born James Murdoch MacGregor in Paisley on February 15th 1925 and moved to Aberdeen shortly afterwards. He decided from an early age that he wanted to be a writer, his youthful ambitions are evident from the start. The earliest work on file is *The Diamond*, a magazine created from a school exercise book in 1938. Other works from this period include *Swing Time for Shakespeare* (1941), a light-hearted time travel story, *None so Blind* (1944), a war story of 214 pages and *Time to Recapture* (1946), a story of 240 pages. What makes these early works memorable is the dedication shown in their execution; they are all written entirely in longhand with a fountain pen.

McIntosh's break came in 1950 when the pioneering American SF magazine *Astounding Science Fiction* published his short story 'The Curfew Tolls', its title a quote from the poem *Elegy Written in a Country Churchyard* (1750) by Thomas Gray. This was a motif of McIntosh and we see quotes from various poets used as titles of other early works: *Some Demon's Mistress* (1950) from Keats; *The Happier Eden* (1950) -from Milton; *Where the Apple Reddens* (1950) from Browning; *A Man's a Man* (1952) from Burns; and *By Any Other Name* (1952) from Shakespeare.

In June 1953 Doubleday agreed to publish a novel by the title of 'X'. They liked it so much that they paid McIntosh a healthy advance but insisted on changing the title to *World Out of Mind*. This was followed by *Born Leader* and then what was probably J.T. McIntosh's most celebrated work, *One in Three Hundred,* a story centred on a dying Earth and the individuals who are chosen to colonise a new planet. The book was reprinted in several countries and was a huge success. A flurry of short stories and novels followed quickly afterwards.

However, just as success was coming into bloom, illness struck. McIntosh entered hospital in December 1953 and remained there until July 1954. The hospital to which McIntosh was admitted specialized in the treatment of non-pulmonary tuberculosis and the duration of his stay also tallies with the treatment of such an illness at that time. But what could easily have become a time of creative stagnation instead became a period of unmatched creativity; during his stay in the hospital he produced more science fiction stories as well as dramas, crime stories, radio plays, a comedy co-written with Talbot Rothwell (a screenwriter who worked on the *Carry-On* films) an unfinished operetta and two volumes of an epic novel (unpublished) set during the Second World War. He also began a detailed correspondence with E.J. Carnell, editor of *Science Fantasy*, on the subject of censorship.

Censorship in the 1950s was a serious problem for publishers of science fiction magazines in both the UK and America, with editors often afraid to publish for fear of ending up in court. McIntosh had at least two stories declined for this very reason. *The Big Hop* was initially turned down by Carnell for fear of upsetting 'the purity league' (it was finally published in 1955). There is also a letter from American literary agent Willis Kingsley Wing explaining to McIntosh that one of his works has been rejected by publishers on the grounds that 'nineteen pages of the story is devoted to unmitigated sadism'.

Around this time McIntosh began an ongoing correspondence and friendship with Robert Heinlein. Heinlein, considered one of the 'Big Three' of Science fiction alongside Isaac Asimov and Arthur C. Clarke, was often outspoken about censorship and shared an interest with McIntosh in glamour/nude photography. McIntosh wrote a book on the subject, *Glamour in Your Lens,* published in 1958. We know from McIntosh's correspondence that Heinlein travelled to Glasgow with his wife in September 1955 specifically to meet him.

Also in 1955 McIntosh struck up a friendship with Edgar Pangborn, winner of that year's IFA (International Fantasy Award) for his novel, *A Mirror for Observers* (McIntosh tied in third place with Isaac Asimov). The two remained friends and the archive includes a letter from Pangborn in 1957 in which the subjects discussed include Johnny Walker Whisky, the town of Kilmarnock, and the works of Robert Burns as well as Pangborn's next move in an ongoing correspondence chess match.

There is also an amusing letter from Willis Kingsley Wing in America at this time asking if there is a problem with the glue on British stamps. This is because all of McIntosh's manuscripts were arriving in America stamped 'Postage Outstanding'. Wing asks him to look into the matter 'as these costs mount up'.

McIntosh's star continued to rise during this decade. *One in a Thousand*, a requested sequel to *One in Three Hundred*, was another big success. McIntosh is also credited with the creation of what is now a universal science fiction term, 'Empath'. This appeared in a story of the same name in 1956 but the archive contains an unpublished, earlier version titled *Three Hours* that predates this by almost a year. However, not everything was going smoothly; a contract to publish McIntosh's work in South America was destroyed when the publisher's proprietor (Juan Peron's former Foreign Minister) was physically dragged from his office and 'most probably shot' (according to a letter from Willis Kingsley Wing). An anthology of his work was planned for the UK market but didn't make it to publication.

The fifties were probably the high point of McIntosh's literary career; his subsequent work began to receive criticism. He was accused of lacking discipline and the archive contains letters from his publishers regretting the apparent rehashing of themes and plots from previous works. His new work increasingly featured beautiful and nubile young women who invariably lost their clothing before ending up in the arms of the male protagonist. There is a letter from Scottish writer and poet, Nan Shepherd, in her capacity of editor of the Aberdeen University Review, in which she congratulates McIntosh on the success of his latest novel (*When the Ship Sank*) but criticises his 'overt focus' on six beautiful women.

During this time McIntosh appears to have grown weary of science fiction; he returned to writing crime stories, radio plays, war stories, television plays and comedy. His crime stories were invariably set in Scotland in the countryside of the Highlands or the Borders. He also moved beyond the world of fiction entirely and wrote books on wine making and cooking. As far as I am aware, none of these works were ever published. Frustration appears to have overtaken McIntosh in his later years and he destroyed many of his own manuscripts and correspondence.

It is difficult to place J.T. McIntosh in the canon of Scottish science fiction writers. As far as genre was concerned, he tended to favour the style of the space opera, with interplanetary wars being a mainstay in many of his works. He also engaged in Time Travel stories, Parallel Worlds, Post-Apocalyptic Fiction, and Robot Fiction. Canadian science fiction critic John Clute wrote of McIntosh that he: 'never lost the vivid narrative skills that made him an interesting figure of 1950s SF, but his failure to challenge himself or his readers in his later career led to results that verged on mediocrity. His early work warrants revival.'

Whilst agreeing with this conclusion, I would emphasise the final five words. Whether McIntosh is to be regarded as a Scottish science fiction writer of distinction is a matter of opinion, but whether he is to be regarded as a Scottish science fiction writer of importance is a matter of *fact*.

McIntosh's skill and imagination resulted in some very interesting, original and pioneering work in the world of science fiction in the 1950s and 1960s. His work deserves to be read.

J.T. McIntosh died in Aberdeen in 2008.

Tony Quinn moved to Edinburgh in his twenties. He worked as a cinema manger for eleven years, including five years at the Edinburgh International Film Festival. Then he worked as an engineer; it was during this time that Tony began a degree in Literatures in English. After the degree he moved on to a Masters and then a PhD on Shakespeare's Juliet (they wouldn't let him do one on Blade Runner). He currently works as an educator and tutor.

REVIEWS

Well here we are, at the start of a new year already. It's been a bumper crop of reviews this last year across the board so I would like to take this time to say a MASSIVE thank you to our plucky team of reviewers. It's an honour to work with you all and your insights have steered us all well through 2019.

Here's the first crop of 2020, and I look forward to sharing more with you.

—Sam Dolan, Reviews Editor

More reviews online at www.shorelineofinfinity.com/reviews

Beneath the World, A Sea
Chris Beckett
Corvus, 288 pages
Review by Joanna McLaughlin

Chris Beckett's Beneath the World, A Sea follows the journey of a British police officer as he tries to uncover the truth behind the murders of a group of psychic human-like creatures. However, disembarking in the other-worldly Submundo Delta after a four-week river journey, Ben Ronson is confronted with an even greater mystery: what did he do during the days preceding his arrival in the Delta which he has lost all memory of? And does he truly want to find out?

While the premise of the novel suggests a move by the Arthur C. Clarke Award-winning author into the world of sci-fi crime fiction, the story can be better described as an exploration of the subconscious and the darkness that lurks within humanity. Indeed, Beneath the World, A Sea, has parallels to Joseph Conrad's Heart of Darkness as Ben becomes increasingly unhinged during his time in the Delta and starts to question everything he thought he knew about himself.

As in his highly acclaimed Eden trilogy, with his new novel

ARTHUR C. CLARKE AWARD
WINNING AUTHOR

CHRIS BECKETT
BENEATH THE
WORLD, A SEA

'Superb... like Conrad's Heart of Darkness reimagined by JG Ballard'
GUARDIAN

Beckett again proves himself to be particularly skilled at creating rich and evocative worlds and complex characters. Indeed, as a reader it was easy to share Ben's feeling of being somewhat hypnotised by the beautiful but unsettling forests that lie within the Submundo Delta, and the enigmatic creatures that live within them.

For readers drawn to fast-paced, sci-fi thrillers this may not be the novel for you. However, for those looking for a thought-provoking novel that isn't afraid to explore some uncomfortable questions about human nature Beneath the World, A Sea is well worth a read.

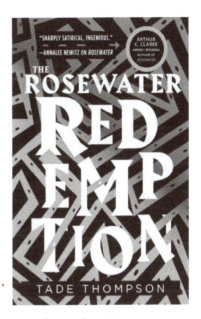

Rosewater: Redemption
Tade Thompson
Orbit Books
Paperback, 374 pages
Review by Joe Gordon

The third and final part of Arthur C Clarke Award-winning Tade Thompson's rather excellent Rosewater series arrives from Orbit, and it proves as engrossing as its predecessors. The first novel introduced us to the world of Rosewater, this unusual near-future Nigerian shanty-town that had grown into a city state, based around a vast alien dome, the power politics going on between locals, such as the city's major, the Nigerian government, the secret police, the aliens and other groups, and the "sensitive" Kaaro and his psychic abilities, which are linked to the alien-created xenosphere. Book two, Insurrection, took us away from Kaaro's point of view and expanded our experience of this world through the eyes of several other characters, less a direct sequel as viewing events

from another angle, giving a much rounder picture of both characters and the history that has lead to this point.

Insurrection also expanded on the alien presence, far from the benign if mysterious visitors who do annual "healing" ceremonies (one of the things which has put the once shanty-town of Rosewater on the political map and made it important) and brought us the xenosphere, this is, in effect, a very slow-motion invasion of our world. It is one which has been going on behind the scenes for decades, centuries even, the base, Wormwood, with roots deep below the Earth. And now more of the aliens are coming from their distant world – or at least the digitally archived mental imprints of that now otherwise extinct species, downloaded into dead human bodies and re-animated in a process similar to the "healing" gifts given to human pilgrims and their injuries.

Jack Jacques, the mayor, has a tenuous alliance with the aliens, or at least a section of them (it appears there are cracks in the aliens and their plans and approaches, just as there are divisions between the different human groups), allowing them to take dead bodies for this resurrection project. Understandably many bereaved families are aghast as this use of the body of their deceased loved ones being used as a vehicle for an alien mind. The arrangement does buy Jacques some bargaining power with the belligerent Nigeria though, still smarting from losing Rosewater as an independent city-state – with the power of the alien behind him, they can't move too openly against Jacques (not that is stops all sorts of backroom plans and schemes).

But this is a delicately balanced situation and not one that can be maintained for long. Nigeria and other powers are interested in what is going on and want to move more openly, laying plans to disrupt the city's routine and destabilise it, Jacques knows also that he cannot rely on the protection of the alien, and even if he could, he understands that each new one that is brought here and downloaded into a former human body is another nail in the eventual coffin not just of Rosewater but for the human race on Earth. He's buying time, but that's all, and he may have less than he thinks – bad enough people are forced to surrender the freshly dead bodies of their loved ones, but what if the belief that the resurrected bodies are entirely blank slate until the alien mind is downloaded are false?

What if there is even a partial imprint of the original human soul still trapped in that revived body, now shunted to the back of the mind as the alien takes control?

A lot of hard decisions are going to have to be made by different powers, all squabbling for their own angle and unwilling to face the fact that perhaps their angle is, in the long-run, meaningless if they don't unite to try and prevent the eventual extinction of their own species and the take-over of our planet by another. Assuming, of course, it is even possible to stop something like this, which has been happening for so many years already, a slow-motion invasion that had established a beach-head long before humans even realise they were at war...

Thompson takes the multi-character angles from the second book and deploys them again here to great effect, giving us insights into the competing human and alien interests, from the ones who are tying to co-operate at some level to the ones who will stop at nothing to impose their own will, consequences be damned (not hard to see echoes of this in, for example, the current climate crisis in the real world and the groups that fight around that despite the dire consequences awaiting all groups regardless of their prestige or power or angle). The notion that the newly resurrected formerly human cadavers, now home to alien intelligences, could also still retain vestigial elements of the original person's mind, their essence, trapped in there, is horrifying, and brings the idea of global invasion to a very personal, individual level, upping the horror element (it is also not hard to compare this to the often brutal colonial/imperial era of history in Africa).

With so much at stake none of the original characters are safe, and there is a feeling throughout of how precarious the lives of even characters we have come to love are, how easily they could die by the hand of the slow alien infestation or by the quicker hand of their own fellow humans still trying to score points for their own agendas. There will be a blood-toll here, and there is a sense of increasing desperation as some of the players start to fully realise the stakes they are playing for, even as they try to form new plans that they have no idea they can pull off. It really is all to play for here, and Thompson immerses us in the situation and in the character's fates – it is a real gut-punch to see something bad happen to some – and keeps us guessing right to the end, how this will play out for both our individual characters and for the fate of humanity and the world.

The Girl in Red
Christina Henry
Titan books 368 pages
Review by: Lucy Powell

A fairytale, but not as you know it. An intriguing take on the classic Grimm fairytale "Little Red Riding Hood", this new novel by Christina Henry is bloody and gripping in equal measure. Whilst the original fairytale is one strewn with darkness, with various tellings of it emphasising or muting the gore, Henry's narrative delves even deeper, drawing out the potential for abject horror like poison from a grizzly wound, and shapes it into a post-apocalyptic disaster narrative.

We follow Red, the protagonist of the novel. Named "Cordelia" after her mother's love of Shakespeare, she has a bright red hoodie and is on the way to her grandmother's house. That much, as people at all familiar with the Red Riding Hood story, we already know. But what makes her portrayal refreshing is that Henry depicts her as a disabled person-of-colour, exploring the prejudice that both bring, even in a society in total collapse. Indeed, as Red walks, treading a fraught and frightening path through the woods and beyond, we are exposed to more of what has happened to bring her there through flashbacks. These nudge the narrative ever closer to the precipice between "real life" apocalypse horror, and sci-fi reminiscent of *Alien* or *Stranger Things*. A nasty scene early on in the novel where she guts a man with an axe promptly makes you aware of what kind of novel you are reading.

Middle America, indeed most of the USA as far as one can tell, is a bleak apocalyptic landscape, with its inhabitants ravaged by an illness for which there is no cure. But the shadow cast by this illness is a darker one, and not - as one would imagine - everything that it seems. Red, and those she travels with, find out more in a painstaking accumulation of tension that is only relieved in the last quarter or so of the novel. Even so, despite the relief, you are gripped with a curiosity about the wider world that, for all its world-building, Henry doesn't quite manage to answer.

The "twist" of the novel is perhaps too jarring for a story that builds itself up to be a more realistic disaster apocalypse novel. Red is a character who constantly reminds herself of the realities of the danger, comparing her actions as separate to those of apocalyptic video games or novels, and so the direction Henry chooses to take with the twist proves to be not as satisfying. Whilst well-written, with an engaging protagonist, the novel seems to straddle two different genres that don't mesh as perfectly as one might like.

Indeed, whilst the apocalyptic plot is familiar, as is the fairytale, I found myself looking for direct comparisons to draw between this narrative retelling and the original tale. The wolf-character, the stalking, vicious, and sometimes charismatic figure to Little Red Riding Hood, is hard to place. Is it the roving bands of militia? The bloodied footprints and dead bodies? The idea that other people in this story are "the wolf", or the fact that this well-known threat is not immediately clear, is one which places a seed of doubt into an otherwise clean ending, reminding the reader that danger is never really far away. A clever, if albeit, weaker ending to a strong, vibrant plot, this novel is still worth reading for fans of "dark" fairy tales and apocalyptic works alike.

Green Valley
Louis Greenberg
Titan books 319 pages
Review by Samantha Dolan

If you came to the Cymera Festival in Edinburgh over the summer after purchasing your Shoreline merchandise, you might have noticed the VR rig in the corner. When I gave it a whirl, it was amazingly disorientating. And climbing up a mountain side and yet not climbing up at all left me feeling slightly nauseous. But I was so buzzed, I couldn't stop thinking about that immersive world and when I could go back in for another try. When I heard about Green Valley, 'a place where inhabitants had retreated into the virtual world full time', I was intrigued.

The story centres around Lucie Sterling. Hers is a 'post Green Valley' world. Much like when the Berlin wall went up, a massive court case that exposed vast corporate corruption sealed the residents of Green Valley inside their virtual reality bunker and banned all technology for those living outside immediately. Lucie has a landline and uses keys and padlocks to secure her home. No smart phones or CCTV at all.

Lucie has a sister, brother in law (David) and niece inside Green Valley but when her sister died, Lucie didn't try and contact her niece, believing that Kira would be safe inside the only reality she'd ever known. But Lucie is a consultant for the police and when she finds out that three dead children could only have come from Green Valley, she realises that she could have been wrong all this time. In the memory of her sister, Lucie embarks on a journey to find out what, if anything, has happened to Kira.

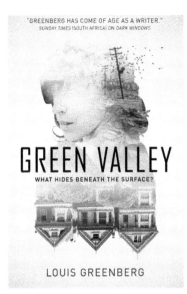

GREEN VALLEY
WHAT HIDES BENEATH THE SURFACE?

LOUIS GREENBERG

There are several beautifully crafted scenes in which Greenberg explains how the virtual reality works. The reader is never allowed to forget that what Lucie is experiencing isn't real, but we're allowed just long enough for the juxtaposition between Green Valley and the bunker in which it 'exists' to be jarring. Technology-free Stanton isn't a Utopia either. There is plenty of political intrigue and scheming within Lucie's police department, that hamper her own investigation. It often feels like Lucie is the only one without an overt ulterior motive as all the antagonists are a heady mix of delusional and self-serving. Through the supporting cast of her partners, both work and romantic, we learn how the world collapsed and how people are creating new lives for themselves. But Fabian, her boyfriend, does sometimes feel like an exposition genie and is little heavy handed. Jordan is also, at times, a little cliched but they really are just there in supporting roles and the nuance of Lucie's characterisation more than makes up for them.

The world building is detailed and delicate and feels very present day which heightens a lot of the tension but it would be overstating things to say that there are too many surprises in this novel. There is a moment where Lucie is forced by David's new wife, to confront just how far from reality David has slipped and it's gruesomely detailed but not ground-breaking. And I think that's my only disappointment with Green Valley. It feels as though it's just on the cusp of showing us a world we've never seen before but just stops short. Being a near future story has perhaps hamstrung the creativity here. But this is a well written, fast paced narrative that doesn't shy away from the best and worst aspects of humanity. It's definitely worth a read.

More reviews online at www.shorelineofinfinity.com/reviews

Apocalypse and Ruins (extract)

Ruins, however ... no, she didn't protest ruins, but when
she issued her injunction
I wondered, What's the opposite of a ruin?
Not merely a functioning building
and bank. It would have to have
a nervous system, sensors in every tile.
Nanocams, -speakers. Advanced ceramics,
the whole structure a 3-D printer.
If you do your job and the boss's too,
the walls grow, vitrify, floor moves you
to a corner suite. Your apartment – convenient,
there – likewise. Or shrinkage,
down to the sub-basement among bunks,
freezers, boilers, sour steam;
everyone within the building till,
suspect or merely unable to pay,
popped from regretful pseudopods
out among the dumpsters, into freedom.
Ruins, yellow wildflowers growing,
roots negotiating stones, pits
where dungeons were and exposed rebar
long vanished, conducive to thoughts
of self and empire seem
more human, in fact essentially human.

Frederick Pollack

Servant's Entrance (extract)

We clone a mammoth. For a week,
hits on her videos outnumber those
for cats. Her fur is a really unique
gold-amber; it inspires fashions
till it starts falling out. Her small, guarded steppe
is the coolest place we could find
but she looks sick and lonely; the amazing
tusks poke disconsolately
at her own dung-boulders.

Those who watch Mammothcam
long enough begin to have
strange dreams. If they're men, they hunt her
through unreal vastness. They're filthy, in great shape,
perhaps overbuilt. Loads of roughhousing
and blood. When they return
to camp, they slap the women around
and demand the largest steaks.
Women dream the same thing.

Frederick Pollack

Frederick Pollack is the author of two book-length narrative poems, *The Adventure* and *Happiness* (Story Line Press), and two collections, *A Poverty of Words* (Prolific Press, 2015) and *Landscape with Mutant* (Smokestack Books, UK, 2018). He has published many other poems in print and online journals.

Prison Ship

The walls are made of glass
so I see into the emptiness of a junk yard,
see without scent of rust or solar panel,
see no airlock, no heat-shield, no docking port;
nowhere to go.

The days are made of waiting
so I feel only numbing penance,
too many days counting down to Earth-side,
too many breaths to force in, out,
nothing else to hold.

The marks are made of runes
so I write but cannot be heard,
write away a scratched-out hope,
write away my fate-forgotten future;
no tomorrow, I beg.
                     But there is no one to beg.

Stone Kissed

From sun to red-end star
time's mason, gravity
will fuse
hydrogen into helium,
carbon flesh into nitrogen earth,
oxygenated water into silicon sand.

Beneath our sun reborn,
on our planet remade,
we will be ground into a monument to the heavens,
polished by a people
whose kiss we will only know
as stone.

Laura Watts

Laura Watts is a writer, poet, and ethnographer of futures. She has spent the last decade researching and writing about tech futures. Her most recent book, *Energy at the End of the World: An Orkney Islands Saga* is published by MIT Press. She currently combines science fiction and poetry with her academic research into energy futures at University of Edinburgh.
Read more on her website www.sand14.com

Magpies

One for sorrow, two for joy.
Three for a girl and four for a boy.
Five for silver, six for gold.
Seven for a secret never to be told.
Eight for uranium, nine for lead.
Ten for the bunker. Eleven, warhead.
Twelve for fallout, thirteen for bones.
Fourteen for vaguely-remembered homes.

Fifteen for magpies, sixteen for magpies
Seventeen for magpies, eighteen for magpies.
Nineteen for magpies, bleached and distended.
Twenty for magpies, slick and segmented.
Thirty for magpies, hunting the weak.
Forty for magpies, with practiced technique.
Fifty for things that we do not discuss.
Sixty for fear they are counting us.

22nd Century Nursery Rhyme

The Wheels on the Bus

The wheels on the bus go round and round
und and round, round and round)
The wheels on the bus go round and round
Don't take off your mask.

The bones on the ground go crunch crunch crunch
(crunch crunch crunch, crunch crunch crunch)
The bones on the ground go crunch crunch crunch
Don't take off your mask.

The guns on the drones go pop pop pop
(pop pop pop, pop pop pop)
The guns on the drones go pop pop pop
Don't take off your mask.

The inquiry on the case goes on and on
(on and on, on and on)
The inquiry on the case goes on and on
Don't believe their lies.

22nd Century Nursery Rhyme

Emma Levin

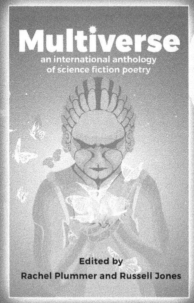

How To Support Scotland's Science Fiction Magazine

CONER '17

Become a Patron

SHORELINE OF INFINITY HAS A *PATREON* PAGE AT

WWW.PATREON.COM/ SHORELINEOFINFINITY

ON *PATREON,* YOU CAN PLEDGE A MONTHLY PAYMENT FROM *AS LOW AS $1* IN EXCHANGE FOR *A COOL TITLE* AND A *REGULAR REWARD.*

ALL PATRONS GET AN *EARLY DIGITAL ISSUE* OF THE MAGAZINE QUARTERLY AND *EXCLUSIVE ACCESS* TO OUR PATREON MESSAGE FEED AND SOME GET *A LOT MORE.* HOW ABOUT THESE?

POTENT PROTECTOR SPONSORS A STORY EVERY YEAR WITH FULL CREDIT IN THE MAGAZINE WHILE AN *AWESOME AEGIS* SPONSORS AN ILLUSTRATION.

TRUE BELIEVER SPONSORS A *BEACHCOMBER COMIC* AND *MIGHTY MENTOR* SPONSORS A COVER PICTURE.

AND .... OUR HIGHEST HONOUR ... *SUPREME SENTINEL* SPONSORS A *WHOLE ISSUE* OF SHORELINE OF INFINITY.

ASK *YOUR FAVOURITE BOOK SHOP* TO GET YOU A COPY. WE ARE ON THE *TRADE DISTRIBUTION LISTS.*

OR BUY A COPY *DIRECTLY FROM OUR ONLINE SHOP* AT

WWW.SHORELINEOFINFINITY.COM

YOU CAN GET AN *ANNUAL SUBSCRIPTION* THERE TOO.

KINDLE FANS CAN GET SHORELINE FROM THE *AMAZON KINDLE STORE*

pic: Joe Gordon

Russell Jones' Prime Jokes

At our regular Event Horizons in Edinburgh, MC Russell Jones unleashes a pack of unruly jokes between acts. He shares his favourite dozen with us now. You lucky readers...

Q: What is it called when Iron Man does a cart wheel?
A: A Ferrous Wheel!

Q: What did 7 of 9 find in Janeway's toilet?
A: The Captain's Log.

Q Why did the martian throw beef on the asteroid?
A He wanted it a little meaty-or

Q: How do you organize a good space party?
A: You planet!

Q: How did Dr Peter Venkman propose to his wife?
A: Bill you Murray me?

Q: How does Yuri Gagarin like his tea served?
A: The milky way

Q: What's spiderman's favourite brand of rice?
A: Uncle Ben's

Q: Which program do Jedi use to open PDF files?
A: Adobe Wan Kenobi

Q: What do you call the robot who loved canoeing?
A: A Row-bot

Q: Why did the robot marry his fiancée?
A: He couldn't resistor

Q: What do astronauts wear to keep warm?
A: Apollo neck jumpers

Q: Who did Frankenstein take to the prom?
A: His beautiful ghoul friend!

Lightning Source UK Ltd.
Milton Keynes UK
UKHW021939170120
357166UK00012B/418

9 781999 333171